WORLD GONE MISSING

Stories

Laurie Ann Doyle

Regal House

Cover photography by Leungchopan/Shutterstock
Author photograph by Laura Duldner

Regal House Publishing, LLC
https://regalhousepublishing.com

Library of Congress Control Number: 2017942122

To Sam and Marco

And in remembrance of Josh

Contents

Bigger Than Life 6

Next Door 32

Or Best Offer 35

Lilacs and Formaldehyde 53

Like Family 65

Here I Am 83

Breathe 103

Ask For Hateman 118

Girls 133

Restraint 153

Just Go 159

Voices 177

Acknowledgements 196

slash it in half, it's still yours

— Ikkyū, *Crow with No Mouth*

BIGGER THAN LIFE

The sycamore leaves outside Ben's window were huge—
bigger than Jack's and my hands put together. I remember
the afternoon light coming off them low and green, reflect-
ing all the veins and hollow places. But the light changed as
it traveled across the room; it had to have changed. Because
when I turned at the sound of Jack's voice, Ben's prescrip-
tion bottles burned bright orange.

"His pills are all there," Jack said. "The antidepressants,
anti-psychotics, and Antabuse."

The room felt hot—the late-May hot of San Francisco—
and smelled of clothes gone too long without washing. I
watched as Jack thumbed through the pages of Ben's books
haphazardly stacked against the wall. He checked the clothes
in the closet: wrinkled button-down shirts and dark pants, a
couple of thrift shop tweed jackets, patched at the elbows.
Ben's tennis shoes sat near the back. They looked immense,
much bigger than Jack's, and run down at the heels. Jack
nudged one with his foot.

"All Ben's things are here," he said. "Only his backpack
and wallet are missing." Jack searched the loose papers on

his brother's desk for a note. He didn't find one. That I'm sure of.

⁊

Driving home across the Bay Bridge, Jack can't stop moving. He tightens his fingers around the steering wheel of the truck until his knuckles turn to sharp points, looks out the side window, stares straight ahead. I look out the opposite window. Beyond the railing of the bridge, a haze hangs over the water, turning the bay an impenetrable green. It's Sunday, so there's no traffic, but Jack switches from lane to lane as if there were.

"What is it, Jack?" I ask. But Jack's not much of a talker and I have to ask again. "Tell me."

"Ben jumped off the Golden Gate Bridge," he says, eyes focused ahead. "Nobody saw it. That's why it wasn't reported."

"What about his belongings?"

"Swept out to sea."

It's been two days since Ben hasn't come home. Why Jack's sure Ben's gone off the bridge, I don't know. But now doesn't seem the time to ask. I lean back against the seat, watching steel beams silently float overhead. Jack's pessimism makes me want to be upbeat. I picture Ben getting off Muni, stopping to buy a CD or take out a book from library, then heading home. Isn't it better to think of him walking up the stairs to his apartment slowly, but still alive?

I've only met Ben three or four times. He's Jack's baby brother and only sibling, someone Jack didn't tell me about right away. Ben's troubled and the two of them really don't spend much time together. Nine years ago—in 1988—Ben moved to San Francisco from New Jersey, where their parents still live.

7

"Hey," I say, touching the bunched sleeve of Jack's shirt. His skin feels warm through the thin cotton. "It's only been a couple of days. Way too early to decide what happened."

I want to go home, back to the house Jack and I just bought on Oakland's Lake Merritt. We're both in our late forties, married for just six months and happy to be starting this new life together. I want to settle into the new corduroy couch with Jack, watch the lights circling the lake come on, sparkling.

"Tom said Ben seemed fine before he left the apartment Friday morning," I say. Tom is Ben's roommate and sometime lover. "Better than he'd been. They chatted over coffee at the kitchen table, remember?"

Jack shakes his head. "Tom sees what he wants to see. When Ben was drinking, Tom thought it was terrific. Round-the-clock party."

"I know. But didn't you tell me that Ben came back that other time?"

"That other time was different, Lucy. Ben went down to Santa Cruz with a friend and forgot to tell anybody. It was just one night. He took his meds with him. His meds keep him stable."

Jack looks over his shoulder in the direction of the Golden Gate Bridge, though we're driving through the tunnel now. Dull yellow lights stream by in a way that makes four o'clock in the afternoon feel like midnight.

"Look, why don't we give it a few more days," I say. "Then we'll...." What? What will we do? Search, of course. But what that means I have no idea. "I'm sure Ben will turn up."

We pass the green sign saying we've entered Oakland, glide down the long slope of the bridge and join the maze of highways going in every direction: north, south, east. And west, eventually.

"Jack?"

"You're right. We should wait. Let's wait." This time when Jack turns to me, his face looks calm. Then I see a tiny twitch at the corner of his eye, something I hadn't noticed before. He presses his lips together as if he has more to say. Nothing comes.

≈

On Saturday, Jack gets drunk. Drunker than I've ever seen him. When I come downstairs for breakfast, glasses sit all over the living room. Some hold an inch of bronze liquid, others just ice, sweating in pools on our coffee table. Trying not to notice, I walk into the kitchen and make coffee. Jack comes in, bringing the scotch. He fills the mug I set out for him and perches the bottle on a cardboard box. We have three yet to unpack. A month ago we polished off a dozen boxes and sat down to a delicious dinner Jack had cooked, garlic noodles and Dungeness crab. Of the two of us, he's the cook. Today Jack stares bleary-eyed at his drink as if there's no one else in the room.

"Hey," I say, touching his fingers. "Are you okay?"

He takes a swallow. "Fine."

Two weeks have passed since Ben disappeared. Jack has reported his brother missing at the police station in the Western Addition near Ben and Tom's apartment; placed classifieds in the *Chronicle, Bay Area Reporter,* and *Guardian*; checked the ERs at SF General and Pacific Presbyterian. Nothing has come of any of it. Every time I offer to help, Jack silently shakes his head. Though he wants to keep searching, Jack remains convinced his brother jumped off the bridge.

When he isn't looking for Ben, Jack buries himself in

work: drafting motions, talking to clients, appearing in court. I'm a middle school teacher, a challenge that often seems easy compared to Jack's profession. He's been a public defender for eighteen years, and is up for a promotion soon. They give him the heavy cases rookies can't handle. But now it's the weekend. Weekends he saves for us.

By noon, Jack's lodged himself in the easy chair by the window, the same chair where Ben sat the last time we saw him. From the kitchen, I start to hear high-pitched sounds that I think must be coming from outside, an animal maybe. When I go into the living room, I see it's Jack. His howling gets softer, then louder and choked with tears.

I sit down in the chair next to him and put my hand on his taut back. He stares sightlessly out our living room window, moving only to touch the glass to his lips. He starts rocking, barely at first, then in heightened swings. His copper-colored hair stands up where his tear-wet hands have run through it; red blotches stand out on the skin of his neck and upper chest. This scares me, but I don't say anything, worried I'll make things worse.

"I should have had him here," Jack says, not to me but the window. "I should have had Ben living with me."

It's still impossible for me to imagine Ben dead. I remember the story my mother told me once, how a distant cousin went around the corner for cigarettes, disappeared, then nine years later walked back through the front door. He was fine. Whole. I picture Ben with a new lover, see the two of them walking together at Baker Beach.

"He'll come back," I say, touching his hand.

"It's my fault," he moans. "I should have had Ben here with me."

"But the two of you could barely spend a couple hours

together," I say before I can stop myself. The idea of Jack's brother moving in bothers me. Ben can be calm one minute, agitated the next. "Didn't you say Ben sometimes drives you crazy? Complaining, or refusing to talk at all."

Jack looks up, eyes rimmed with red. "He was my brother. I should have taken care of him."

Our conversation circles like that for hours. By early afternoon, I'm yelling, "Jack, please stop drinking!" He pours himself another scotch.

I go outside, water the pot of yellow chrysanthemums, a housewarming gift from a friend. I come back in, gather up the mail, distract myself with recycling.

Suddenly I'm outside again, driven by frustration and upset. I walk up the highest hill above Lake Merritt, pushing hard. The mind-numbing exertion feels good. I pass century-old Victorians and modern apartment buildings, pick my way along a sidewalk buckled with roots. At the top of the hill, I turn and look at the bay. This afternoon the sky is a deep fogless blue, unusual for the Bay Area in June. The Golden Gate Bridge appears in the center of my view, an unnatural bright orange.

I don't look at the dark specks that might be people, walking or biking or doing whatever it is they do on the bridge. I don't imagine Ben hurling himself off. Instead I stare at the arches pointing toward the Embarcadero, the Transamerica Pyramid, the immense tower of 555 California Street. I want San Francisco to open up, let me see into its narrow alleyways and twisting streets, discover where Ben is. I want him back with every cell in my body. Because with Ben comes Jack, and my world. Or at least some part of it.

Back home, I sit on the couch and try to get Jack's restless brown eyes to meet mine. Maybe if he talks, gets it out, he'll feel better. His eyes brush past to places unknown. He stands up, wanders out of the room. He comes back in, sighs. Our house fills with Jack's sad breath.

That night, I lie down next to the man I love, barely able to touch his restless body. He rolls on his back, flings out an arm fitfully. Sighs again. It's as if Ben had moved in with us, only he's not there.

❧

The first time I met Ben—fifteen months before—nothing seemed wrong. He looked handsome that night, his collared shirt a shiny green and his gray slacks ironed to sharp creases down the front. He wore black dress shoes.

Standing next to Jack in the doorway, I saw how much bigger Ben was, not just tall but big—bigger than life that night—even his hands were huge. His face was full and the skin smooth; his sunglasses gave him a sophisticated air. Jack looked like the younger one, his body compact, but thin. The two of them didn't seem like brothers.

Jack had invited Ben to his apartment—a large, empty one-bedroom in the Rockridge district—to meet me. After a dinner of rib roast and baked potatoes, Jack went to clean up. Ben and I stayed in living room, finishing our coffee.

"So what do you do, Ben?" I began awkwardly. Jack and I had known each other just a few months but the relationship was already serious. I'd never met anyone in his family and wanted to make a good impression. Maybe talking about our jobs would be a good place to start. "For work, I mean—"

"You know, Lucy," Ben interrupted. "Jack has told me virtually nothing about you. Why don't you begin?"

"Me? Okay. I'm an eighth-grade English teacher. At Claremont Middle School over on College."

Ben frowned behind the dark glasses he'd never taken off. "Eighth grade," he said. "Now there's a high point in human existence. I admire you."

"Oh, it's not bad. The kids are great. Most of them, anyway. A few try to make my life miserable." I remembered Jack had said Ben's problems started in middle school. Eighth grade hadn't been the easiest for me, either and I felt a wave of empathy. "How about you, Ben?"

"I'm working at the Federal Reserve Bank."

"That's right. I remember now Jack mentioning that. On Market Street."

Ben nodded. "Though working would be the wrong word. Slaving away in their dungeon mail room is more accurate." He laughed, and after a moment, I did, too. "But the truth is I just gave my notice. I've re-enrolled at San Francisco State. Computer Programming."

"Wow. That's great." Jack had warned me that Ben might talk incessantly about some trivial detail, even abruptly walk out of the room. But the man sitting next to me on Jack's couch was polite and clearly intelligent. I saw confidence in the set of his broad shoulders, a confidence I hadn't expected, and that reminded me of Jack. "Good luck."

Ben's smile was so big I could see his perfectly even front teeth. "Thanks. I'm pleased. They don't accept just anyone."

We continued talking, moving easily from topic to topic: Clinton's chances for re-election in November, Microsoft's Windows 2.0, the Stones' new *Voodoo Lounge* album. I leaned back on the sofa, thinking, *You know Jack, your brother's all right. Maybe he's turned a corner.*

Jack appeared in the archway that separated the living and dining rooms. "How's it going in here?" he said. "Did

I hear laughter?"

"Good. It's going good," Ben said, coming to his feet. "You don't have any more cake, do you?"

"Sure." Jack smiled. "Help yourself." He turned and went back to kitchen.

Instead of following Jack, Ben veered down the hall. I heard a door open, the toilet flush, coughing, another flush. When Ben reappeared, without any cake, his grin was wider and his eyes looked bloodshot. He stood above me and began to talk, making big sweeping gestures that sometimes brushed my shoulder. He started in on French intensive gardening, switched to marijuana cultivation in Humboldt, then jumped to something about the light whipping across the Pacific in the dark.

"In the dark?" I said.

"You know, the Coast Guard."

"Oh," I said, completely lost. "That's right."

Ben looked down at me, his eyes hidden behind the dark glasses. "I know you know." He rocked back on his heels so hard the wood floor creaked. "Happens all the time." I nodded and inched away from him on the couch.

When I looked up, Jack stood in the archway again. He glanced at me, then at his brother. "Ben," he said in a calm voice. Then, loudly, "Ben!"

Ben kept talking. Jack made a sound through his teeth, a long breathy sigh, something I'd never heard before. "Cut it out, Ben," he said. "You're ruining everything."

Ben's stream of words didn't stop.

"Ben, are you listening?"

Ben scowled. "I'm not ruining a thing. I'm chatting up your new girlfriend."

"No. You're blathering."

"What do you want me to do?"

"I don't know," Jack said, exasperated. "Tell her about the dinosaur."

Ben sat down. "Okay. So," he said, turning toward me. "We drove up to Trenton—"

Jack listened for a few moments and left. Soon Ben was talking about how far Trenton was from south Jersey, and how slow his mother drives, only that day it'd been worse because it was snowing and ice had frozen Route 1, and she kept forgetting to turn off her blinker—here he paused and waited for me to say Go on—and did I know the turn signal was a relatively modern addition to the American car, that's why his father had to keep flicking it off. He and Jack in the back seat could scarcely breathe because the windows were rolled up, all their cigarettes, five packs a day between his parents...

This time I was able to follow—barely—but minute after minute ticked by and still he hadn't mentioned a dinosaur.

"Excuse me," I said, the next time Ben paused to take in a breath. "Maybe I'll just see if Jack needs help in the kitchen."

"Good idea," Ben said, following me. Our evening ended soon after.

The next morning, Jack told me that, growing up, Ben had been the star.

"My brother could master anything," he said.

In first grade, the teacher discovered Ben reading the front page of *The New York Times*, which was taped over the glue table. At nine, he taught himself algebra. A year or so later he focused on science. In the Trenton museum, he identified, in Latin, some misclassified dinosaur bones. He wrote the museum directors, who sent back their congratulations.

"My mother framed the letter," Jack said.

But something changed in adolescence. Ben couldn't keep friends. He'd phone and yell at the teachers now failing him. He began seeing psychiatrists, first by himself, then with the whole family. Doctors diagnosed Ben with a thought disorder, said he was bipolar, then paranoid schizophrenic. Two months before graduation, Ben dropped out of high school. He'd lost his ability to focus, forgot the math and languages he'd taught himself as a kid.

"Maybe it was the meds." Jack sighed. "The Risperdol, Elavil, Zoloft, Thorazine. And those are only the ones I remember."

༞

After that scotch-filled weekend, Jack emerges as if from a dreamless sleep. He stays sober, is up and out of bed before I open my eyes most mornings, already downstairs planning where to search next.

Jack stops cooking. We eat store-bought sandwiches, and sometimes a miserable-tasting mac and cheese I've tried to fix. If he sits down, it's not to eat, but to study a torn map of San Francisco, or phone and check with the police. Something will surface, I tell him. It has to.

Jack takes days off work to search, visits Ben's favorite bookstore in the Haight, talks to men in line at Saint Anthony's soup kitchen. When I ask if he wants company— carefully, because a single word can catapult him away—Jack nods, then leaves the house without me.

The phone rings and rings. At first I run for it, breath caught in my throat, thinking it must be Ben, or at the very least news. But it's Jack's mother Rosie, who talks to me only for a moment before she wants Jack. They spend hours debating where Ben is.

Or it's Tom, who asks if anything's turned up. When I tell him no, he's still cheerful. "That boy's coming back," he says. "I'm sure of it."

My mother calls occasionally. My parents divorced long ago and we don't talk all that much. "Oh honey," she says. "Think positive."

I take on a couple of summer school classes, grade student papers, reread them, revise my comments. Alone, I unpack the last of the boxes, find a place for the potholders.

A month after Ben disappeared, Jack remembers Dan Moore, a law school classmate who, instead of taking the bar, opened a private investigation firm in Potrero Hill. Jack calls his parents and they decide to hire the man.

Moore energizes the search, spreading it in concentric circles from Ben and Tom's apartment on Broderick Street. He tacks up flyers with color photos—Ben sitting on the plaid couch drinking a beer, petting his cat Boris, the headshot from San Francisco State—on telephone poles and bulletin boards all over San Francisco. He and Jack visit more police stations and talk to precinct captains, making sure every investigation procedure is followed.

The police haven't shown much interest in Ben's disappearance. Hundreds of people go missing in San Francisco every year, they say. Most come back on their own. They haven't searched Ben's apartment or conducted interviews. On their own Moore and Jack check inpatient psychiatric units and jail holding facilities. Ben hasn't touched his bank account in five weeks, but Moore remains optimistic.

"Just a matter of time," he says.

Leads start coming in. A woman on Ashbury Street is sure she saw Ben at her Saturday garage sale. The groundskeeper at St. Mary's reports a man fitting Ben's description. Jack and Moore check John Does at the county morgue. None of this information goes anywhere, but they're sure something soon will.

In mid-July, the phone rings after dinner. I'm upstairs planning lessons and let Jack answer. I hear the familiar greetings, and silence. Then Jack's voice rises with excitement.

"Really? You're certain?"

After he hangs up, Jack sits down close to me.

"Looks like Moore's located him," he says. "Some guy living in Golden Gate Park described Ben to a T. Same height and build. Same black hair."

Jack's eyes hold mine for the first time in weeks. "Will you come?" he asks. "I want you there." For the first time in weeks, Jack is excited, smiling.

I smile back. "Of course."

Early the next morning, Moore meets us in the Panhandle. The three of us walk through the eucalyptus trees to Golden Gate Park. Moore glides ahead in his hiking boots, blonde hair flying around his head. Jack walks next to him, matching Moore's pace. I hang back, feeling a strange mix of happiness and dread. I want to find Ben. I'm also afraid of what we might discover. Ben could be incoherent. Or want to stay missing. Run off. I push away these thoughts and catch up with Jack. I reach for his hand.

The entrance to Golden Gate Park off Stanyon Street is full of bright green trees. Teenagers with safety-pinned eyebrows sit in a circle on the lush grass. Nearby, a man wrapped in a ragged blanket spins, singing loudly to himself. As we get closer, he eyes us warily. Moore bends downs and shows a woman in black the photo of Ben with his cat. She shakes her head. A man with a grizzled beard next to her leans over and points to a dirt trail through the pine trees.

"He says he saw Ben last night in an encampment. Back here," Moore says.

"Let's go." Jack walks quickly in that direction.

We cross mounds of fog-damp earth and flattened pine needles, see an overturned shopping cart half covered with a sleeping bag. A tongueless shoe. Flies swarm around a lump of shit.

Jack's shoulder touches mine as we follow Moore down the path. We come upon a Styrofoam cooler spilling its contents: a hypodermic needle, two metal spoons, a coffee cup filled with mud. Moore pushes ahead through the tall weeds, leaving us there.

"Hard to believe Ben could be living like this," Jack says. "What about his meds?"

"Maybe he wants to try life without." A blurry picture rises in my mind, Ben walking purposefully, unhampered by regimens and side effects. It's a picture I hardly believe myself.

"Jack! Lucy!" Moore shouts.

He's motioning to a circle of people in a clearing. A few dirty faces turn toward us. A woman with open sores on her cheeks stands and runs off. A man with thick black hair keeps his back to us. It's Ben's hair. We cautiously make our way toward him.

Don't bolt, Ben, I think, both nervous and exhilarated. All these weeks of worry, of not knowing, are over.

The man looks over his shoulder. His hair is hacked back to dark fuzz, a mustache merges with a beard. But his red-veined eyes are dark green instead of Ben's blue. When he suddenly comes to his feet, I see he's shorter, by at least half a foot. A slice of white belly hangs over his pants. Ben is big, but not fat.

"What is it?" the man says, fear in his voice.

"We thought you were—" Jack pauses. "Someone we know."

"Here." Moore pulls out a five-dollar bill. "For your trouble." Faces look up. He hands the man a flyer with Ben grinning at its center.

"Thanks, man," the man says, stuffing it into his pocket. "Who is this guy?"

Moore explains. "So call me if you see him," he says. "There's something in it for you." He looks around the circle. "Any of you."

When we walk back to the Panhandle, Jack lags behind. Every time I stop and wait, he looks farther away.

A battered truck roars past, spewing a cloud of gray-brown exhaust. My eyes sting. For the first time, I let doubt enter my brain. Maybe we will never find Ben. But what happened? He has to be somewhere.

Jack's face narrows with worry. The story about that distant cousin of mine comes into my head. I remember my mother saying it was as if he dropped off the face of the earth. Nine years, nothing. Then out of the blue, he reappeared. Just like that. Hope trickles back in my brain.

"It's a good sign," I say, turning to Jack. "Finding that guy. Means we'll get other leads. Means we're close."

Moore nods.

Jack stares at the sidewalk.

॰॰

The last time I saw Ben—three days before he disappeared—he walked as though the air itself was too heavy to push through. We'd invited Ben over, along with Rosie and Sid, who'd flown in from New Jersey, to see our new house.

A celebration, of sorts. I was standing at the window when Ben walked up from the bus stop. Instead of forty-three, he looked seventy. His hair ran in gray streaks from his forehead, his shoulders were hunched. He'd buttoned his plaid shirt wrong and only half tucked it in, giving his body a lopsided look.

I opened the door. Ben smiled faintly and hurried toward the chair by the window as if he couldn't sit down fast enough.

"The doctor has me on a new medication," he said when he caught me staring. He spoke openly, unashamed. "We're hoping it'll settle me down enough to drive. I'd really like to learn how to drive." He wiped away the sweat that had gathered in the lines of his forehead, though the afternoon had turned cold. The fog that had swallowed San Francisco was now streaming across the bay.

We'd planned a barbeque before the weather changed, so now we huddled in the backyard. Sid sat in a lawn chair away from our picnic table. Jack concentrated on grilling the chicken. Rosie, a short woman with champagne-blonde hair, smiled and sat down next to me. Ben hung back, finally placing himself across from his mother. Rosie and I began chatting about the haircut she got yesterday near Union Square, Nordstrom's shoe sale, the trip to Sausalito she and Sid had planned for tomorrow. Before long the conversation dwindled.

"Need any help?" I called to Jack, hoping he would. He shook his head.

When I turned back to Rosie, she was whispering. Ben stared down at his hand splayed on the table as if it might do something menacing if he looked away. Sweat slid down his neck.

"Sweetheart," Rosie whispered, "How are your classes going?" And when Ben didn't answer: "What about volunteering at the museum like we talked about?" and "Ben, let me send you some new clothes, shirts and Dockers. Macy's new fall shipment is coming. What colors do you want? Blue might be nice, or green. You always liked green."

Ben glanced occasionally at Rosie, nodding or shaking his head, not eating the chicken on the table, just sipping water and staring. Sid watched him, shifting in the flimsy chair, his black glasses dark against the skin of his temples.

Finally to no one in particular, Sid said in a loud voice, "Look at him, would you. Just sits there." He paused. "Like a moron."

There was a stunned silence.

Rosie said, "Sid, please—"

"Back off, Dad," Jack interrupted. "Ben's trying."

"A complete *moron*," Sid said firmly. He was staring, too, but unlike Ben, his eyes were sharply focused, the muscles in his jaw clenching as if he had more to say.

Ben kept his head down, didn't say a word. When he looked up, his face seemed blank. Then I noticed a slight smile, as if he were saying, *You see. You see what he does.* He continued to look out at us with that calm, strange smile.

I wanted to yell at Sid for being cruel, make him apologize. Without a word, I looked from face to face to face. In spite of the fog now blowing in clouds across our backyard, I felt warm, Then hot. I drew in a long cool breath of detachment, felt it slide down my throat. This is not your family, I told myself. Stay out of it.

༔

In September, Rosie calls Moore from New Jersey and fires him after nine weeks' work.

"For Christ's sake," she says. "He wanted to charge us for two ten-foot phone cords, a staple gun, an hour's worth of time for walking to the copy shop. Five thousand four hundred and sixty-two dollars all told. You tell me. Where are the results?"

So now it's just us.

Though us would be the wrong word. Fewer and fewer weekends Jack drags himself out of bed and makes the drive alone to San Francisco to search. Ben's been missing three months. Jack goes to bed early, sleeps ten, eleven hours at a stretch, and still looks exhausted. This worries me, but when I ask how he's doing, Jack simply shrugs.

Jack's asked for and been given a lighter assignment at work, though nothing's really light in the public defender's office. The date for the promotional exam has come and gone without Jack signing up. I find scraps of crumpled notes lying on the kitchen counter or bathroom floor in Jack's tilted cursive: *Call Officer— Get high school— Map to—* None of them is finished.

Days go by. We pass each other in the kitchen and bedroom, make small talk. At school, I find myself irritated by kids who never would have bothered me before. At night, I cook, or try to—easy stuff like tacos and pasta—scour the pots till they shimmer, take out the garbage. Half-eaten containers of yogurt and blackening banana peels reappear on the kitchen counter. I clean up, again.

Then—that's it. I leave the full-to-the-brim trashcan in the sink, just to see how long it'll take for Jack to notice the odor. Three days go by. Fruit flies circle the kitchen.

Finally I hand him the bin. "Be my guest."

Jack looks confused. "What? I just took it out."

"Are you kidding me?" I say loudly. "You haven't done a

thing in three months!"

Then I'm yelling—how I've been holding everything together, cleaning, paying the bills, cooking even. Jack yells back he is helping. Helping. Working. Trying to find Ben— "Get off my back, would you!" Our voices spiral louder and louder, weeks of frustration spilling out.

"All right!" Jack shouts. "Go ahead. Take over!"

I stop and stare at him. "What?"

"Take over the search. You think it's so easy."

I almost say he's not my brother. "But I have no idea where Ben likes to go. Or do."

Jack smiles, a faint smile, but the first I've seen in weeks. "You want to help? So help. I'm tired." He turns around and takes the garbage out.

I'm full of ideas. We'll expand the search, put ads in different papers, contact outlying police stations. I'm more energized than I have been in months. Then it dawns on me. Ben could be anywhere. Moore focused our search in San Francisco, a city we know well. But maybe Ben's taken off for Tijuana with a new buddy, except no one can locate that man either. Maybe Ben hitchhiked to DC, or is living in a New York City subway, or panhandling in Venice Beach to throw off anyone checking his bank account, which he still hasn't used. The possibilities are endless.

I don't know where to start. When I admit this, Jack nods like *Yeah.* We sit down and, in the longest conversation we've had in months, decide to cover the places Moore gave low priority: residential stretches in the Sunset, Marina and Inner Richmond. We spend a long afternoon stapling flyers to tarry telephone poles, talking with people mowing front lawns and getting out of Subarus. We leave flyers in espresso bars up and down Fulton Street.

Rosie continues to call three or four times a week. Now she wants to talk with me. "Anything yet?" she asks.

"Not yet."

"Have you thought about LA?" she asks. "Ben visited last summer, he loved the palm trees. Maybe he decided to see San Diego. Beautiful this time of year, I've heard. What do you think—you, Jack, a nice trip south. Our treat?" We laugh.

"Lucy." Rosie's voice is suddenly serious. "How are you doing?"

"I—" No one has asked me that question in months. Colleagues at school no longer bring up Ben's absence, assuming, I suppose, if there's news, I'll share it. When my mother calls, I tell her what I tell Rosie now. "I'm okay."

"This isn't what you bargained for."

"Oh, I'm holding up. It's harder on Jack."

"I'm glad Jack has you. Sid and I both are. Family's important at a time like this."

"Thanks," I say, and mean it.

Sid never comes to the phone. Sometimes I hear muffled voices in the background. "Rosie. Please. I can't."

⌒

In November, a woman from the Omni Service Center in the Sunset leaves a message on our machine. She's seen someone like Ben and wants to meet in person. Jack and I rush off in the car but traffic on the bridge slows our pace to a crawl. It begins to drizzle, then the skies open up. Water pours in sheets down the windshield, hits the car in sharp blasts. Jack's breath comes in heavy exhalations and soon the windows cloud. When we finally reach the center, the woman has left for the day.

"Ben might show up," Jack says in an emotionless voice.

"We should post flyers." He hands me several.

"Where?"

"Think I know? Ask."

The front-desk clerk behind the glass partition barely glances up. "Over there," he says, tilting his head toward a yellowing hall.

Over there takes me to a wall-size bulletin board without an inch of space left. Dozens of missing people stare out. Some of the flyers are curled and faded. Others boast color photos so new they glare. A father sits smiling with a baby in his lap. His shirt is bright green, matching the little girl's one-button sweater. A photo of a black-haired man with '60s sideburns and thick glasses is tacked up next to them. Below is a teen-ager posing in a glittery prom dress, his hair swept in an updo, one hip playfully stuck out. Danny was last seen two weeks ago, Lloyd, six years. Bill would be twenty-seven now.

I suck in a breath. It's not just Ben. None of these people stand in the doorway, sit down to dinner, take the bus home. A whole wall of blank space left behind. I realize there are bulletin boards like this all over the country. Hundreds of thousands of people go missing every year, I've heard— enough to fill cities. I'd always ignored the gap-toothed kids pictured on milk cartons, the blurry photographs at the bottom of circulars. Now I stare. Where is Ben? Where could his spiraling thoughts have taken him?

Jack walks over. "It's so crowded," I say. "I can't find room."

"Come on, Lucy." He grabs a flyer out of my hand and in one brusque motion tacks it up. The corner covers the pink cheek of a woman last seen in 1990, seven years ago. Jack looks down the hall toward the front door.

"Why don't we check Stern Grove?" I say. "Didn't you

say Ben sometimes went there? Maybe we'll find some sign of him."

Doing this doesn't make a lot of sense, but doing nothing seems worse. We make our way out.

The east side of Stern Grove is vast, full of dirt ravines and tree-lined pathways. Jack moves ahead. I stop and look up. The sky's a deep November blue now, beautiful to most people, but ugly to me. To me, it looks like an empty, waterless expanse. The pines nearby are spindly, their branches hanging and still. The only muddy footprints I see are our own. I try to imagine Ben strolling, sitting on the bench close by, leaning back to read a book. I can't. Our trip to Golden Gate Park five months before, how lush it now seems, how full of life. Bright, disgusting life. A wind spins dead pine needles in loose circles. People with their backs to us are better than no people at all. I long for stained sleeping bags, a tipped-over cooler, a torn shoe. I want to go home. What's the point?

"Let's try over here." Jack zigzags up an embankment energetically and suddenly I'm right behind him. It feels good putting one foot after another, much better than staying still. I'm not thinking, not moving in any definite direction. But not aimless. Not that.

At the bottom of the ravine, Jack and I stand with our backs to one another, looking in different directions. I sigh but Jack stays quiet. As I turn, his hand grazes mine, our fingers touch. His palm feels cool and flat and wet—from sweat or rain, I can't tell. The skin warms. We walk back.

❧

So much continues without Ben's body. When the balances on his credit cards come due, Tom sees they're paid using Ben's disability, which continues rolling into their joint account. Tom keeps up Ben's share of the rent, sends the minimum on his school loans. When Boris, Ben's cat, meows, Tom feeds him and refills the water bowl. Tom and Rosie talk on the phone two or three times a week, brainstorming where to search next, ideas they pass on to us. Neither of them wants to look, but both urge us to.

The fact is we're searching less than before. We keep meaning to, telling each other *Let's check the Sunset again, and the Panhandle.* Jack sporadically visits police stations and morgues. I don't ask for news.

It's January, seven months since Ben disappeared. Sometimes a bill collector calls about accounts we don't know Ben had. The man argues Ben's alive, just hiding out.

"Been gone that long. Really?" he says skeptically. Seems they've heard stories about missing family members before. I stop answering the phone altogether.

Ben is now my loss, too. He's a hollowness Jack and I pass between us. Sometimes the emptiness brings us together. *You're here,* Jack's eyes seem to say. *You haven't gone.* Other times I can't stand the silence; even looking at the chair where Ben sat before he disappeared hurts. I buy new cups and serving spoons, just to put away the ones Ben had touched.

Sometimes I want to leave, do leave, and for too long, thinking maybe I'll never come back. I spend time in places Ben never would. The Embarcadero ice rink where the skaters endlessly circle. The carousel in Golden Gate Park where the music reaches for you long after you've left. Still Ben finds me, slips in when I'm least expecting, his sloping shoulders, splayed hand, moist forehead. I see a dented green dumpster, half-hidden by bamboo, and I can't help but imagine Ben lying behind it. His hair's red where it should be black, an awful dried red. Maybe he just left for an hour or so before whoever it was did whatever they did to him. Maybe Ben didn't want to go missing. The world's full of strange violence and—I don't finish the thought.

Loneliness seeps under my collarbones, fills my breath. Suddenly I'm on the bridge driving home, steel girders gliding by. Jack's not angry when I walk through the door. He doesn't hover, doesn't follow as I hang up my coat or put down my purse, ask me where I've been, worried. Sometimes his eyes flash a soft hello. Sometimes he hardly looks up.

৯

The day after Labor Day, Tom phones.

"Forgive me," he says. "Could you... come get Ben's stuff? I've rented out his room." Ben's disability stopped three months ago in June—a year after he disappeared. There's no money to pay Ben's rent.

"Come by anytime," Tom says. "I'll leave a key under the mat."

The next Sunday, we knock on the apartment door. No one answers. Jack cautiously slips the key in the lock.

"Hello?" I call. Silence. We move toward Ben's bedroom, a place neither of us has seen in fifteen months.

The threadbare jackets are still squeezed between the wrinkled shirts, Ben's big tennis shoes sit back in the shadows. Someone has taken a Cognitive Science textbook from the stack against the wall—you can see the gap—and left it on the bed. Otherwise, the room looks untouched. The same gray walls, clutter. On Ben's desk sits a metal box I didn't open before. I lift its lid. Inside, all but two of the black-and-white photographs are unfocused, fuzzy images you think will become clear if you look long enough, but never do. One has crisp dark edges of a man standing outside a tunnel in Golden Gate Park. Another is of Boris stretched out on a braided rug, one eye closed. I discover a souvenir San Diego shot glass with a penny stuck in it.

Jack looks around. I numbly bend down and begin to work. Packing is a chore I've done dozens of times; I helped Jack when we bought the house. I've always liked it, this wrapping up of life in one place in anticipation of the next. Where's the next now? I fold a pair of Ben's extra-large T-shirts and stack them on the bed. I bundle together tube socks and lay them together like pale eggs. All of Ben's belongings have a musty, old-man smell.

Jack moves slowly, but I work faster and faster, wanting the whole thing over with. My hands take on a life of their own. I don't put similar possessions together, don't tape the boxes shut. The shelfless books—murder mysteries and computer texts—get mixed up with Ben's tennis shoes. I wrap wadded Dockers pants that Rosie must have sent around a chipped coffee mug. Ben's reel-to-reel tape deck sits next to a leaning stack of tapes, the labels dusty and peeling: U2, Coltrane, Mozart. There's no cassette player. Except for a pill bottle that's fallen, Ben's prescriptions still sit lined up on his desk. Jack scoops up the translucent orange containers and tosses them in the trash. I open my mouth to protest, then stop. Ben's medications have to be expired by now.

We run out of boxes and carry belongings down in our arms. "You okay?" I ask Jack as we pass on the stairs. He nods an unconvincing yes. I lay Ben's things inside Jack's pickup shell, go back for more.

Finally we finish. Ben had more to pack than we'd expected. Afterward, Jack and I stand on Broderick Street alongside his truck. He leans back, stares up at dry sycamore leaves, and ejects a long stream of pent-up breath.

"Hey," he says, "that was a blast." We both crack up.

But Ben's possessions won't let me go. I stare at his belongings strewn across the rusty pickup bed. Ben's dress slacks lay twisted around a black shoe, the pages of a paperback are torn. Suddenly I want to cry: open, breathy sobs. I lean against Jack, who takes my weight. I press my face into his warm neck. Only a few tears come.

"Let's go," Jack says. "We're done here."

But we're not done, we're never done. Driving home across the bridge, things slosh back and forth behind us, as if they'd roll that way forever. As we cross into Oakland, I ask, "What are we going to do with all Ben's stuff?" Our house is full of everything we've bought together over the past two years, too full.

Jack glances at me, then stares straight ahead. "I don't know," he says.

NEXT DOOR

She walked into the kitchen, crumpled to her knees, and died, her daughter said.

Our houses have stood side by side for more than a century. The walls are so close I can reach out and almost touch her windowsill. We share a narrow driveway. Standing at the kitchen sink for the first time sixteen years ago, I saw the face of the woman next door appear at her window in our mutual slice of morning sun. She was plucking out chin hairs. From upstairs, I watched her reposition pots of white cyclamen on her front porch, sop up rainwater with thick towels. At ten every night, the bedroom light switched off. At six in the morning, the toilet flushed.

Her name was Esther. She was tall and thin and wore hats. Big beige bowls for gardening, tightly woven black straw for opera and church. If I stopped to say hello, she'd complain that weeds from our side had spread, that maple leaves were littering her yard—her blue river-stone and moss, grass-free front yard. The wrought iron fence surrounding it rose to sharp black points.

"My husband put in this fence, you know," she told me more than once. "My husband, you know, was chief of staff at the hospital before he passed. So if you ever need any medical attention, let me know." I took to parking our car on her side just so we'd have something else to talk about.

Three years ago, Esther phoned out of the blue. "You like martinis? Because if you've got the olives, I've got the Bombay." My husband and I drank Blue Sapphires and watched the A's game on Esther's new twenty-four inch TV. Big, she bragged. Her house smelled like cat litter and cough syrup.

"That was fun," she said afterward as we stood out on the porch. "But bring a light bulb next time, would you? I could use an extra." We laughed, but there was urgency in her voice. As if she wanted to make certain we'd be back—soon. When our son was born, she gave him a silver cup with his name engraved across it. "Every boy needs one," she said with no further explanation.

Six months ago I suddenly saw hands in Esther's bedroom window, pale arms reaching but no head. Cars I didn't recognize parked in our driveway. A sister, one neighbor said. Then, a nurse. Another nurse. Doors slammed. The toilet flushed at all hours.

The last time I saw Esther, she stood inside her black fence. "Hello shoes," she said as I walked closer. She'd piled stones in the corner of her front yard, only half burying the yellow-flowered sour grass that had sprung up. Her face was so wrinkled it looked scarred. When she asked me when her birthday was, I made something up. She smiled, waving to my feet as I left.

Two days after Esther died, a different daughter came to clean out the house. A son rode up in a white motorcycle, put the cat in a crate, and drove off. I watched cardboard boxes being carried down the steps, handmade pottery bowls and flabby cushions. After the daughter left, we went through the pile left out on the sidewalk for pick-up. When no one was looking, I took the Christmas present we'd given Esther years before—a stainless cocktail shaker still in its red box—and an unraveling roll of *fleur-de-lys* shelf paper.

Two weeks ago, a couple with a baby due next month moved in. An upright piano sits on the front porch and the bedroom light comes on and goes off whenever it wants. This morning I caught the woman next door—the one I've never met—staring at me as sun filled the glass of the window. I looked away, looked back, but still she was staring. As if my face, too, might suddenly go missing.

Or Best Offer

A woman stood in Lowell's driveway, her head glowing. The skin was so perfect and smooth— not a bump or nick anywhere—that he inexplicably shivered. Of course, he'd seen plenty of men with shaved heads before, but never a woman. This one had hair elsewhere, lots of it. Wild un-plucked eyebrows arching like wings, red-brown patches under her arms, a fine blonde down her legs. The breeze played with the hem of her dress.

He stepped closer. Her eyes were pale green.

She smiled. "Tell me about the car."

"Well, it's out back here." Lowell walked her around the stucco two-story to his backyard where the Ford Taurus sat in the tall grass, the car's color so faded it seemed to blend with the foggy August air. She was the third person to come by to look at the 1994 Taurus, a car his wife brought to the marriage eighteen years ago and left when she moved out in March. He wanted nothing more than to be rid of it.

Lowell stood by the passenger door and opened it. The smell of something spoiled—an apple core maybe, or beer left in an empty—drifted toward him. He quickly opened the driver's side, too.

"Runs great," he said. "Take a look inside. Roomier than you'd think."

She propped her bike—a pink cruiser with thick white-walls and a silver basket—against the house and slipped off her backpack. Instead of walking to the car, she sat on the steps next to a pot of dead marigolds—something else Sarah had left—and for a moment turquoise panties flashed before her dress fell between her knees. "Isn't it kind of old?"

"Old isn't necessarily bad," he said, his fingers going to his hair. Once it'd been a thick brush of black. Now it was white, a pure unruly white that made him feel older than forty-seven, hair that people said made him look distinguished. Distinguished—*that* he hadn't felt like in months. "The car's reliable. That's what I'm trying to say. The engine's got only sixty-six thousand on it." Okay, seventy-five, but close enough.

She tilted her head in a way that made the skin gleam.

"We could take it around the block, if you'd like. A test drive?"

The woman wandered now over to the Ford without a word. She peered in the dusty windows and ran her finger gracefully over a long scratch on the passenger door. "What happened here?"

He shrugged as if he couldn't remember. "Got keyed, I think." The afternoon had started out as one of those well-meaning trips with Sarah to Crissy Field. Within an hour, he was driving around Ghirardelli Square screaming at the windshield. Doing things he'd later regret, like dragging a sharp key across the side of the car.

The woman nodded as if she understood. "What's the

trunk like? I need a big trunk. I haul a lot of stuff."

Lowell wanted to ask her what kind of stuff, but stopped himself. All the junk he'd discovered getting the car ready to sell had been tossed back there: Styrofoam takeout boxes, a plastic bag of Sarah's bras and pajamas destined for the thrift shop, his faded copy of *Great Expectations*.

He fingered the keys in his pocket but didn't bring them out. "Trunk's roomy, too."

"Great." She smiled and looked around the narrow yard. Lowell's shoulders rose a little. This he couldn't hide: the grass so high it'd turned to straw and seed, thick ivy vines threatening to pull down the fence. Dead needles from the pine trees in back buried what was left of Sarah's impatiens.

"Your yard's cool," the woman said.

"It is?"

"Yeah, wild." She picked a long blade of grass and ran it lightly up her arm. "Grown out."

He found himself grinning. That she liked what he'd ignored so badly for the past six months appealed to him more than he expected. The yard had been Sarah's domain. Something she spent hours planting and fertilizing and fussing over, especially after they gave up on having children. Became *child free*, as people put it. Only it wasn't free. She'd pull him outside for long discussions about princess flower versus angel's trumpet, a clover mix instead of grass.

When they were first married, he'd loved the way Sarah could examine something from every possible angle, talk on and on. Then it began to drive him crazy. It was easier to let Sarah decide which plants and exactly where, while he did the grunt work, the digging, hauling, and mowing. They'd worked outside in the garden last August. This summer, he avoided the yard altogether.

The woman did a little spin on her toes. "The car's good," she said, looking right at him. "I'd like to buy it."

"Wouldn't you like to drive it first? See how it runs?"

She shook her head—her beautiful, naked head. "It's just what I want. A good, reliable car. Not big. Not small. The mileage's decent, right?"

"Not bad," he said. A lot of Fords got worse.

"Awesome." She rummaged in her backpack and brought out a slip of pale blue paper folded in thirds. "Here's a thousand."

He should have known. "The ad says two. I've a copy here in the house. The Blue Book is closer to three thousand. It's a fair price. More than fair."

"You're right. Absolutely. It's just—" She squinted as though the light coming through the pine trees was too bright. "Can I pay you in installments?"

Lowell handed her the check back. "Sorry. It's my wife's car, really. We're separated, you know, and it's tricky—"

"I'll give you half today and the rest next week. You can keep the car the whole time." Her arm floated over her head and Lowell found himself staring at the tuft of reddish hair. "Just don't sell it."

"Can you get me cash?"

"Cash is totally fine. Really. I'll run to the bank. Be right back." The next thing he knew, she and her pink bicycle were rolling down the sidewalk.

"Hey," Lowell yelled, but the woman kept pedaling. "Wait!" He didn't even know her name.

❧

The phone rang half a dozen times. Usually he let calls roll over to the muted answering machine—his cell got lost months ago—but at the last minute, he decided to pick this one up. Maybe it was someone else calling about the car. The woman with the shaved head had never returned. It'd been a week and a half and the Taurus was still sitting out there in the weeds.

"Any luck?"

Sarah. She phoned once, maybe twice a week, usually when the boyfriend was out. *No reason we shouldn't talk*, she'd said. *No reason we can't be friends.* He'd agreed, at first thinking no problem. He missed Sarah sometimes, all her energy and deliberate decision-making.

"No, not yet," he said.

"Maybe we should lower the price. What do you think? It's been three weeks. Nobody wants American cars anymore. Not that I completely blame them. A Taurus isn't exactly exciting. You put OBO in the ad, right? In bold?" The car was technically Sarah's property, but she'd offered to split the money down the middle if he did the selling part. And he could use the extra thousand to pay for the big screen he'd bought.

"Of course." Actually, he hadn't.

"You cleaned up the yard, too, like we talked about? Mowed the grass so it'll show off the car?"

"Tell you what, Sarah. Let's change the ad. List your number."

"Okay, okay, Lowell. But don't you think we should lower the price? I know you're going to say the Blue Book's a good third higher, but it's taking an *awfully* long time. Let's face it, the car's old. All scratched up."

Wasn't she the one who'd thrown the keys at him? Who'd yelled *Go ahead!* He'd been standing close to the car and his arm had seemed to fire by itself.

"Hello?"

"Look, Sarah. The car's going to sell. We just need to give it time, is all. " He hung up.

After a minute, the phone rang again. This time he didn't even go near it.

❧

The blinds in the kitchen sagged. One side splayed crookedly, the other tightly bunched up. After breakfast that next Saturday, Lowell went yet another time to try to fix them and the whole thing fell off at his feet. The sun shone through the dusty windowpane for the first time in months, illuminating the big white kitchen. He'd told Sarah he wasn't moving out.. Absolutely not. She could live wherever she pleased with that balding sociologist of hers, but he was staying put.

Lowell leaned toward the window now, his heart racing.

Out in the yard was the woman with the shaved head circling the Ford, her legs looking longer he remembered. He opened the door and walked out on the back steps, forgetting he was just in his plaid boxers.

She smiled and waved. "I called, you know. Like a billion times. You never called back. So I just came over. You haven't sold the car, have you?"

"Didn't you say you'd be right back?" He'd given up days ago.

She kept smiling. She was wearing a short black skirt and white lacy stockings that made her thighs look pale and muscular. "I left you a message. Messages." She held out a thick envelope. "It's all there. Go ahead, you can count it if you want."

"It is?" Lowell stepped onto the wet grass. "The whole two thousand?"

"No, silly. The whole *one* thousand. Sorry it took me so long. We've been in rehearsal."

He opened the envelope slowly. "Rehearsal?"

"I'm a dancer."

"You mean like ballet?"

"No." She did a little pirouette and landed with her feet turned out and heels touching. "Modern. But not Martha Graham modern. Trisha Brown modern. We have a company in the Mission called Pull. Maybe you've heard of it?"

"Awesome." He had no idea who she was talking about. "Sure you don't want to go for a test drive?" He imagined her sitting next to him. What would the air smell like? Jasmine?

"How about we go for coffee?" she said. "I'm dying for a cup."

When the waiter at Emporio's in Union Square asked if he'd like a Mimosa Tangelo Special along with the double cappuccino, Lowell said *Sure, why not.* He wasn't all that great at talking with people he knew, much less with people he didn't. Flagg said she'd like one, too.

Flagg—that was her name, she'd told him. Two *g*'s.

Lowell hadn't sat this close to a woman in months. When he asked her how she ended up with that name, hoping for a good long story that would let just him sit and look, watch the light move across the silvery skin of her head, watch the people who turned to stare, too—Flagg just shrugged.

"Oh, I saw it somewhere. On a book, I think. But it was almost something else. United, or Like, or Scab."

"What was your name before?" Lowell asked, signaling for another mimosa. They'd only started talking, and here was the word *scab*. He didn't know what to make of it. A word that could mean a lot of things—hurt, healing, betrayal. And he didn't know what to make of the tiny holes working their way around Flagg's earlobe and up the delicate rim of her ear. They were filled, randomly it appeared, here and there with green studs. Emeralds, he decided. But faux or real, he wasn't sure. One flashed in the sun.

"Before? You mean what was I born with?"

He nodded.

"Jane."

"You are definitely not a Jane."

"Thank you for noticing." She leaned across the table and kissed him gently, drawing his tongue towards hers. "Not everyone does. What about you?"

He fumbled for his glass and when he finally got his hand around it, took a good long drink. He held the champagne in his mouth until he felt it fizz against the back of his skull. He took another swallow. He looked not at Flagg's head now, but her breasts. They were high and round, a nipple outlined in a soft strip of sun. The skin over her collarbones glowed.

He made himself look away. "Nope," he finally said. "No Jane here."

Flagg laughed. "Come on. How did you get the name Lowell?"

"I grew up in Kentucky," he said as if this were the explanation. "My father's people were preachers. Lots of Lowells before me."

In college, he'd stayed away from girls like this. Flickering smiles, skin so shiny it looked combustible. Now he felt an attraction he couldn't—and wouldn't—ignore.

"Could I ask you a question?" he said, motioning to her head. "Why do you do it?"

"Shave?" Flagg waited for him to nod before going on. "One day I thought why not? The worst, I figured, was I'd have to let my hair grow back. That was four years ago. I like it, I do. How I feel every breeze and raindrop. How people look." She turned to show him the back of her head. At the base of her neck was a pink patch of skin—birthmark maybe—that, as Lowell stared, took on the shape of people dancing. Two or three, maybe.

"How do you think it looks?" she wanted to know.

"I think it's nice." He emptied the glass. *Nice.* God, that was original.

"So it's my turn to ask you a question."

"Didn't you just ask me one?"

She smiled like it wasn't funny. "Why did you break up with your wife?"

That he hadn't been expecting. At work when people asked, he told them they just needed time apart. Nobody was talking divorce. When Bradley in the office next door pressed, Lowell said things hadn't been good for years. He doubted Flagg would let him get away with anything so vague.

Still he stumbled. "Hard to say exactly. Both of us got busy elsewhere I guess." That wasn't true. He'd never been busy, his decades-long job at the San Francisco Public Library a clock-in-clock-out affair. It was Sarah's life that was the whirl. Dinner meetings, the Y, girls' night out. Or so she said. If their marriage wasn't working now, she'd told him, then when would it? He thought what they had was okay. "My wife was the one who called it quits."

"I'm sorry."

"Don't be." He sighed. "Probably for the best."

"Still. No fun."

She leaned forward as if she were going to kiss him again. When she didn't, he sank in the chair, looking down at the wrinkles in his white T-shirt. The loneliness was the hardest, whole weekends when *Grande, extra foam* and *Have a wonderful day*, was it when it came to conversation.

"No," he admitted. "Not fun."

"Hey—it's not over yet, right?" Flagg said. "Right?"

When he didn't say anything, he felt her looking at him, a look he couldn't quite read when he raised his eyes. Sympathy, maybe, or a sort of curiosity.

"You're sweet, you know. And nice looking. Really."

"Thanks," he said. "You, too."

"Say," she said, raising one eyebrow. "You wouldn't want to go someplace, would you?"

He sat up. "Aren't we someplace?" It wasn't completely a joke. He hadn't been in Union Square in years, the for-once fogless sky a vivid blue. The palm trees ticked in the wind and people surged, smiling and carrying shopping bags. A woman stopped, pointing up at the goddess on Dewy Monument. Here was pretty good. Hell, here was great.

Instead of laughing, she ran a finger up his arm. "I don't know. It's crazy, I know. But crazy can be good. What do you say?"

"Sure." Lowell's heart flung itself across his chest. "I mean, that would be fine—" He paused. "Another time. I've got to go pick up my kid. Saturday afternoons he's mine."

He felt more embarrassed than scared driving back. Well, scared, too. The yard was one thing—*wild* maybe if you were feeling generous—but inside the house was a complete disaster. After Sarah had left, he'd felt the rooms separating, floating apart as if nothing held them together. He'd unfolded the futon, left it permanently taking up half the living room, and pushed the coffee table alongside it. He'd gotten so he wanted everything close, pressing in. The books he was reading—or trying to read—lay scattered across the dining room table and chairs. Books, he'd always loved. Not those digital things, but real books with their cinnamon-smelling pages, books you feel the weight of. Six months ago, he couldn't get a book thick enough, not just Dickens, but Bolaño, Tolstoy. Now all he did was flip pages, reread the same sentence he'd just reread. After work, he punched on the TV. Around the screen sat grease-stained pizza boxes, tortilla chip crumbs, and a stack of Tecate cans still indented where his fingers had pressed in.

Flagg parked the Taurus in front of the house, and switched off the engine. "That was nice," she said, giving him a big smile. "Thanks."

Lowell opened the door and pressed his foot on the curb, but didn't get out. He was still feeling a little drunk. "I'd invite you in, but—"

"I know, you've got your kid."

"We'll see each soon, right? The last payment and everything?"

"Right." She looked at him. "Lowell, please don't take this the wrong way—but you don't actually have a son, do you?"

"I don't?" He went to shut the door, hit his foot, and winced. "I mean, how did you know?"

"If you had a kid, I'd see a bike, a football, something on your steps, and in the car. Children have a ton of stuff. They leave it everywhere."

Lowell tilted his head back on the seat. "You're right. We never had children. It's just— This is all so new. Meeting people. You."

He wanted to tell her he didn't always lie. No. Not at all. He had just wanted the car to sound good. Not perfect, but fine. That was how he hoped she'd see him, too. Not someone old and messy and unable to have children. But okay.

No, more than okay. Great.

Fat chance now.

"It's actually way less complicated without kids, don't you think?" Flagg said. "For everyone concerned."

"I guess." But he found something hopeful in her words. Like she was one of the concerned. He eased himself out of the car and stood alongside it, waiting for Flagg to appear on the other side.

She walked around and handed him the keys. "I'll just get my bike." But instead, she stood and looked up at the white trail of a jet spreading across the sky. "Where's that headed you think?"

The cloudy tip was already blurring. "I don't know. West. Japan?"

"Now there's a place I've always wanted to go." She kissed him, but one of those get-in-and-get-out kisses now, her lips firm. She ran her hands over her head as if she were smoothing back hair. "I'll call you, okay. Soon."

"Okay." Even that much kiss had his breath coming faster. She didn't smell like jasmine at all, but clean, wet dirt.

Ten days later, he called her cell. The outgoing message immediately switched on: *Hey you. I'm out there having fun. Where are you? Tell me.*

"Flagg," he said so loudly it surprised him. "I think you know who this is, Flagg, but in case you don't, it's Lowell. I can't wait forever, you know. Other people have shown interest, you know." He was about to say he'd put the ad back up online and was going to keep her thousand dollars, but at the last minute hung up. After he'd said Flagg the second time, he'd gotten hard. He thought about jerking off. Instead he stood at the window and watched a bird light and shit on the car.

"Right," he said. "Join the crowd."

He walked outside, picked up a mildewed cardboard box, and put it in the garage. He hosed down the car and drove it further back in the yard. He tossed Sarah's dead flowers in the compost, threw away a rusty trowel he found stuck in the dirt. He knew exactly where the lawnmower was but made no move to use it. Now he liked the look of the wild grass, the white-headed dandelions spreading across the lawn, the hairy nettle leaves, the pointy anise he used to clip down. He walked to the pine trees and grabbed handfuls of dead needles and brought them inside.

The afternoon was cool and fog coming in. He threw bunch after bunch of brown needles in the fireplace and lit them. Flames shot up and sweet sap-smelling smoke filled the room. He tossed one match in after the other, and felt good. A fire in August! Something he'd always wanted to do. Something Sarah would have hated. Lowell looked around the room with satisfaction.

That's when he noticed the answering machine light was on and blinking red.

&

Flagg appeared in the doorway of the bathroom wearing nothing but a white T-shirt. Lowell sat on the kitchen floor naked. His hands had been everywhere under that T-shirt, on the nipples pointing at him now like sweet hard buds, in her softness below. He looked down fondly at his penis.

"Come over here, you," he said.

"Are you sure you don't want to? A lot of women find it sexy."

Lowell shook his head. He'd always been proud of his full head of hair. Besides, what would they say at work? "I don't think I can."

Flagg took his fingers gently and touched them to her scalp. She had a stiff blonde growth now, shadowed a honey color in back. He remembered it brushing against his chest, the edge of his ear.

"It'll look cool."

His neck felt loose. What had she said? It'd grow back. What else? *It's not over yet.* No, not by a long shot. Maybe it would look cool. Anyway, she'd like it.

"What the hell," he said, a smile spreading across his face. "But first things first."

"You mean, second things." Flagg slipped off the T-shirt and lay on top of him, circling her arms around his head. He licked her armpit. It smelled flowery, not deodorant flowery, but like the bitter smell of real flowers. She sucked his ear-lobe and the skin of his chest. He lifted his head. She had the most amazing breasts, pale and full, with surprising dark nipples.

Afterward, Lowell rolled out from under her and across the linoleum floor. He kept rolling over and over on its cool hard white surface. When had he last made love twice in the afternoon? He'd been worried he wouldn't even be able to get it up.

"You," he said, "are wonderful and strange. I can't get enough of you." He nuzzled his body up against hers.

"You're pretty nice yourself, guy." Flagg stood and walked into the bathroom, still naked. He heard drawers open and close, a latch click open. Knowing she'd be coming over this afternoon, he'd vacuumed the entire house, even scrubbed the bathroom tile. But he hadn't cleaned the inside of the rusty medicine cabinet, hadn't cleaned the inside of anything.

The rummaging noises continued. "We'll need a sharp

razor," she called. "Don't you have one?"

Now he stood in the bathroom, nude too. Flagg held up something bronze-colored, something he faintly remembered from years back. A graduation present, maybe, something way before Sarah, for sure.

"Let's use this," she smiled. "Nice new blade." The razor gleamed under the florescent light.

"This isn't going to hurt, is it?" Before the words were out he knew they sounded wimpy. Suddenly he felt old.

"Shouldn't," Flagg said matter-of-factly. "Not if we take it slow." She turned on the bathwater and spread a towel across the floor.

"Sit here," she said, pointing to the edge of the tub. "And don't move."

Using the scissors she'd found somewhere, Flag clipped Lowell's hair close to his head. She tilted his head right, and left. He tried to suck his stomach in, then gave up, letting his flesh take its usual folds. Her arms moved around him, softly, efficiently. Hair fell into small piles, white strands floated in a breeze he didn't feel.

"Okay." She shut off the water, stepped into the porcelain tub, and sat down. "You can lean back on me if you want."

Lowell eased himself against her. Her breasts felt smooth and damp, the air steamy. She splashed warm water on his head and lathered what was left of his hair. Then in smooth, firm strokes, he felt Flagg taking it down to skin. Bits of hair landed on his shoulders and slid down his neck. He pressed himself closer. Without thinking, he reached back to itch and felt the razor catch.

"What happened?" he said.

"You moved."

"It stings." He imagined a bright column of red running down his back, the water turning the awful color of blood.

"Just a nick. Happens."

He felt a thumb pressing firmly into the back of his head.

"It's stopped. Really," she said. "You're more sensitive now, that's all. The skin's exposed. But—" She lifted her hand away. "We can stop anytime. Just say the word."

Lowell touched his scalp, sliding his fingers down the greasy-feeling shaved skin and the remaining strips of bristly hair. When he brought his hand back, only a spot of lather was tinged pink. Nothing hurt now. But what if his skull was shaped funny? What if he had all kinds of weird freckles? A mole? Bumps?

"Are you okay?"

"Yeah," he said. "Keep going." Some sort of strange mohawk would be much worse.

In a few minutes, Flagg was done. They stood up together and brushed hair off each other's thighs and feet. It was sticky. She ran her lips lightly over his scalp. "Perfect. Just that one spot."

She stepped out of the tub still nude. When Lowell didn't follow, Flagg flashed a look of irritation. "Don't you want to see what it looks like?"

He made himself walk to the mirror, sure he'd hate what looked back. He closed his eyes. When he opened them again, a face he didn't recognize hung there. His scalp was pale and so shiny it had the look of sun on water. His fingers glided over it.

"What do you think?"

"I like it," he said, surprising himself. It was as if pounds had been lost. Who cared what Bradley at work thought.

"I knew you would." She came behind and pressed her

body into his. He felt her moist breasts again, the hard knot of one nipple. "Sooner or later."

Two naked heads looked out of the mirror. Two heads he thought looked terrific together.

"Next time I'll do you. That'd be fun."

When she averted her eyes and didn't answer, Lowell knew he'd done something wrong. "Or not," he added hastily. "No big thing."

She pulled away, went into the kitchen, and slipped on her T-shirt. This time he followed. He opened up the refrigerator and felt a rush of cool air around his head.

"Would you like me to fix you some eggs? I make a mean mess of eggs."

She still didn't answer.

All he had in the refrigerator was a bottle of vodka, a few eggs, and two pickles in lime green juice. He'd meant to go shopping before she'd arrived—pick up a baguette and some cheese, maybe a bottle of good Chardonnay, but had run out of time cleaning. He'd even changed the bed sheets, never imagining they'd end up on the kitchen floor.

"How about a nice Smirnoff scramble?" Lowell turned enough to see her smile and look away.

"Can't. Got to go."

He jiggled the door of the refrigerator, making himself wait this time before he spoke. "Have a rehearsal coming up?"

"Two in fact. We're doing new work." Flagg stepped into her panties and slid them up her legs. "You know, Lowell. I like you. I do. You're funny. And nice." Instead of smiling, she frowned. "I just don't think I'm your kind of girl."

When she didn't continue, he asked slowly, "What kind is that?"

Her eyes went to the top of the refrigerator where a dusty photo of Sarah and him stood. One that had sat there so long he never saw it anymore. Her hair was poofy and sprayed, his so shiny and black it looked wet. Their shoulders pressed tightly together.

"I don't know," she said, staring at the picture. "*That* kind, I guess."

Stay, he wanted to plead. *Just a little bit more. Spend the night. The week. Tomorrow morning.*

"Hey, you still owe me a hundred dollars." His attempt at a joke sounded lame. Yesterday Flagg had stopped by and given him nine one-hundred-dollar bills. They'd made plans to get together this afternoon. Now Lowell watched her zip up her skirt and strap on beaded sandals. His head began to pound as he closed the refrigerator door.

"It's okay," he said. "Take the car. It's yours."

Flagg walked up close to him. "I'll mail you a check. Tomorrow. I promise."

He looked at her. "No. It's fine."

"How about the bike?" She touched his arm. "I could give you my bike."

"A pink cruiser?" He walked down the hall to the closet and put on a blue shirt and shorts. After Sarah left, he'd moved all his clothes in there so he could avoid the bedroom altogether. "No thanks."

"Well then." She reached for her backpack.

On the front steps, Flagg kissed him behind his ear.

"That's so much easier now," she said, smiling. Lowell smiled, too, a little. His fingers went to the slippery skin of his head. He watched her drive away in the scratched up Ford, the car he once so desperately wanted to get rid of. It turned at the corner and disappeared.

Lilacs and Formaldehyde

Late at night I heard my mother cleaning, the roar of the old Hoover, the sound of chairs scraping across the floor. Smells of Lemon Pledge and sudsy ammonia wafted into our bedroom.

"Zach, do you hear something?"

"Not really," my boyfriend grunted. "Maybe."

"What's going on?"

"Beats me." He rolled over and fell back to sleep.

My mother died five months ago. She'd had high blood pressure, high cholesterol, high everything, doctor appointments all the time. Last January, she beat back double pneumonia and was her old self again. Calling me two, three times a day, wanting me to come over and fix the TV, check the checkbook, dust. The last time she phoned she asked me where the Kaopectate was and I told her in a not very patient voice. Then, feeling guilty, I offered to bring over chicken soup. She was my mother, after all. And I, her only child, my father long gone. She pulled in a raspy breath. "No, I'm fine. Really. It's nothing." She didn't sound very happy either.

That night my mother died in her sleep. Quickly, the doctor said.

Now here she was furiously cleaning our apartment. I heard her humming "Stormy Weather" and talking to the furniture the way she always used to when she rearranged it. "Not bad," I heard. Then, "Old friend."

I didn't want to go see. Maybe her face was decayed and half crumpled in, maybe she was just a bodiless voice, a vacuum running through air. Maybe she looked the way I remembered her when I was a child, just five foot three, but *huge* to me, with a long, pale neck and eyes that went from brown to green in bright sun.

In life, cleaning had not been her thing. Rearranging furniture, yes, but never cleaning. She'd sponge the kitchen counter in big, fast circles, leaving a thick rim of crumbs. Before Zach and I moved her into the senior facility, I had had to scrub congealed blood out of the refrigerator meat compartment. Now I heard my mother washing dishes with a vengeance at three in the morning.

Something crashed. Then, something else.

I was out of bed in my pajamas and bare feet before I knew it, heading into the kitchen. She had pulled out the garbage can and was standing alongside it, holding a Blue Onion plate up to the light. Soapy water dripped down her Playtex-gloved finger.

"That's my plate," I said. Actually my grandmother had given it to my mother, who'd given it to me.

"It's cracked, Emma." She threw it in the trash.

"What are you doing?"

"Can't be eating off cracked plates." She looked at me long and hard. Her hair was back to its original dark red. In the glare of the kitchen light, two flushed spots of mauve stood out on her blue-white cheeks. She wasn't wearing the black pantsuit we'd buried her in, but turquoise slacks and a bright gold sweater still covered with Esmeralda's cat hairs.

My mother dragged on her Pall Mall until it glowed. Apparently she had decided in death she could start smoking again. The long ash tipped, but didn't fall.

"It was only chipped," I protested.

"Could have cut you." Her voice had that stubborn Fresno twang it could get. She dunked a milky glass in the foamy water with the same intense energy I remembered.

Growing up, when my mother had turned all her attention on me, life seemed magical. She'd take me to her office on Van Ness and proudly introduce me around like I was the smartest kid in the world, and to Golden Gate Park where we'd float silver balloons up until the treetops glittered. I would play dress-up in her evening gowns and pointy high heels, shiny fabric pooling around my feet. But long gray months went by when she ignored me. Babysitters picked me up right after school and stayed way past dark. Even my mother's toothbrush was missing, away at the office.

As adults, we fought and made up on a regular basis. Had I tipped the waiter enough? Was this really the best parking spot? Sometimes whatever I did wasn't good enough. But we shared a closeness, too, from hours in bookstores where she'd head off to history, and me to art; holidays lost in shopping on Union Square.

Right after my mother died, memories kept coming out of nowhere: her sunburned hands setting a picnic table in Yosemite, the salty smell of Rice-A-Roni, her red-lipsticked mouth opening to the green olive of a martini. Sometimes I'd forget she was dead and pick up the phone to call. I missed her more than I'd expected.

But lately, whole days went by when I barely thought of my mother at all. Zach and I started going to movies again at the Metreon, rediscovered the tacos at Señor Sisig's. I thought I'd finished grieving.

"Why are you here?" I asked.

She held another heirloom plate up to the light.

"Stop." I reached out and touched her arm. My hand didn't go through. Her skin felt cool and firm, something between damp clay and moist cement. Smoke drifted around her blue cheeks. My mother put down the plate, stubbed out the cigarette in an old rosebud ashtray she must have dug out from a box somewhere, and reached into the cupboard. She pulled out one of my favorite mugs, the one with *Emma!* and a green dog painted on it that she'd made for my eleventh birthday.

"Not bad," she said, "don't you think?"

Suddenly I was crying.

My mother, Joan Frances Trotter, had been one of two women in her architecture class at Berkeley in 1958. She'd studied long and hard, but married quickly. "Turns out what your father really wanted was a homemaker," she once told me, "which I had absolutely zero interest in becoming. So that was that." I don't even remember him. What do I do remember is how invincible my mother had seemed. She'd been good at math, good at drawing, and so persuasive that she talked the principal at best high school in San Francisco into admitting me, despite grades that were "fair to middlin,'" as she put it. As an adult, I wondered if I'd ever measure up. There seemed nothing my mother couldn't do.

Even rise from the dead.

"Honey, it's all right," she said, wiping my tears away with a dishtowel. She picked up a spaghetti-stained dish and shooed me off to bed. Sniffling, I went.

The next night I lay awake for hours, listening intently. I'd doze, wake up, listen. In the dark, the silence felt overwhelming.

Zach wasn't fazed by my mother's reappearance. "Happens," he said. He didn't see my mother, but never questioned that I had. Zach spoke about life after death as fact, Elvis being just one example.

As weeks passed, I wondered if in fact I'd really seen my mother at all. Maybe my mind had been playing tricks. Life with Zach slipped back to normal, breakfasts of oatmeal and English muffins, the rush off to work, dinners out occasionally, and concerts at The Great American.

One morning, I caught the scent of Jean Naté cologne. There was my mother floating above our living room couch replacing the burned-out bulb in the overhead light fixture. The sun poured through our now dust-free blinds. Her hair was not red this time, but white, a bright, too-shiny white. Her sienna-colored fingernails were carefully manicured, something she'd never gone for in life. She was wearing a sleek, aqua pantsuit—she'd loved pantsuits since Katharine Hepburn first appeared in one—belted with a delicate silver chain.

I hadn't imagined a thing.

Task completed, she drifted down, her black high heels digging into the couch cushions.

I thought I'd be happy to see her, but all I felt was annoyed. "Mom, you can't just waltz in here any old time you want. I have a life."

Without responding, she stepped off the couch and scrolled through her phone. In life, she'd never had a cell, just a big boxy PC, which she'd used well into retirement. She'd liked to redesign wings of famous buildings and email the plans to old colleagues. "Keeps my hand in," she'd said.

"Mom, you've come back after death," I said. "Why can't you just fix the light with a flick of the wrist? *Pouf!*"

She kept scrolling.

After my mother had died, I sat next to her for hours, waiting for the hearse. Esmeralda the cat slept pressed close to her body, even after she'd turned cold. I watched an earlobe turn pale blue, her cheeks sink. I felt grateful for how quickly she'd gone—without long months of suffering—not only for her, but for me, too. Her phone calls, though frequent, had never come in the middle of the night. She hadn't taken to walking into the elevator wearing only her bra and panties, or leaving the gas on, like other women I'd heard about. My mother had organized garden tours, visited people in the hospital, and started a book club in the residents' library. She had kept her wits about her until the end. Well, mostly. When I cleaned out her apartment, I did find a pile of gigantic half-eaten Baby Ruths and a wad of lipstick-streaked Easter napkins carefully rubber-banded together in a kitchen drawer. Sometimes her smile looked blank. But my mother had never socked me. Never slept with the gardener and written him five separate one thousand dollar checks, like her neighbor down the hall. My mother died quickly and easily.

Or so I'd thought.

Now she looked up from the phone. "Emma, I'm worried about you. I mean, what kind of life are you living?" she said. "Really?" When her tongue darted out to lick her lips, it looked moist and dark.

"Mom, I'm fine. Zach and I both are."

She gave me one of her looks, the one that said *I don't be-*

lieve a single word you're saying. Okay, so at thirty-nine, I hadn't quite hit my stride yet. I'd always loved art, had hopes of becoming a painter. But there was the matter of a day job. So far I'd cashiered at Whole Foods, stocked shelves at Amoeba Records, and sat huddled inside a cube inputting data in the netherworld of Bradford, Newton & Smith LLP. Long months sometimes stretched between gigs. Luckily, Zach and I lived in a rent-controlled apartment in the Haight. Beautiful, small, cheap.

"*Tempus fugit,*" she said.

"Mom." It had been one of her favorite expressions. Time flies, is fleeting, is gone before we know it.

"You know, that's what I said, too. Right before. 'I'm fine.'"

I stared at her.

"But I wasn't. When I phoned you my heart was stabbing my ribs so hard I thought it'd burst out my chest. It wasn't Kaopectate I needed, but an ambulance. I didn't want to scare you. Scare myself, really. I was sure if I kept saying everything was fine, it would be. *Surprise.*"

"Oh, Mom." So dying had not been easy.

"You think it's fun lying around in a grave? I worry. I wasn't the best mother in the world, but I'll make it up to you now. Emma, you used to have dreams. Art, creativity. What happened?"

"I'm fine, I told you." The last thing I wanted was my mother bossing me around again, telling me how I'd fallen short. Zach had said he was a little worried, too—my insomnia, the way I walked around, distracted. But I wasn't about to tell my mother that. "You can go ahead and die for real now, Mom."

"Hah!" She waltzed out the front door.

෮

Walking dogs in Golden Gate Park—my current job—wasn't all that great, but it wasn't all that bad, either. The park was lush year round, filled with luminescent tree-ferns and peach-colored roses, even in December. The fog smelled like ocean. Nonie, Duff, and Cleo, the pugs I was responsible for, were slobbery but sweet. Yes, it got boring sometimes. But the work also left me plenty of time to do other things. Not cleaning—I hated cleaning—but preparing paintings as big as walls. I had old sketchbooks filled with line drawings. But so far I hadn't done much in my spare time. Judge Judy was a lot more interesting than people gave her credit for.

Zach didn't mind that I hadn't found myself yet. He went faithfully off to the Sports Basement every morning, a job he said he loved, helping kids pick out sturdy shin guards and unpacking fresh A's baseball shirts. I believed him. It was my mother I didn't understand. After she died, I discovered a stack of overdue bills and scattered bank accounts. I'd always thought she was supremely competent, organized in every way. But after I'd paid all the bills and funeral expenses, not much was left. Enough so that dog walking didn't have to be an everyday thing. For now, anyway.

෮

The smell was no longer Jean Naté, but lilacs and formaldehyde. Pall Malls. I'd see a flick of red hair, or feel a strong presence just over my left shoulder. I'd rush out the front door, peer down the diamond carpeted hall. "Mom," I'd call. "Are you there?"

Nothing.

Small things started to seem significant: a quarter moon perfectly centered in our bedroom window, a line of black ants trundling along the edge of the sink. It was as if my mother were trying to tell me something. A cricket chirped behind the living room couch, the couch my mother had floated above a month before. I heard foghorns on clear days. My mother loved foghorns.

Our mantelpiece was crowded with photos, but now I saw only the ones of my mother. I turned them face down. I didn't want to look at the scalloped black and white of her standing at Berkeley's Sather Gate, eyes serious, one arm thrown jauntily up in the air. Or see me pressed against her thigh on my very first morning of kindergarten, drowning in a much-too-big backpack. Or stare at a faded Polaroid of the two-story she'd designed on Potrero Hill. A house that no longer existed.

No more middle-of-the-night cleaning extravaganzas, just strange little incidents. Books tidied on my nightstand with the one on Frida Kahlo jutting oddly out of place, an iridescent-eyed peacock feather stuck in a cracked vase— evidently cracked was now okay—a box of oil-pastels stacked among the dinner plates. I tucked the box away, promising myself I'd do some art soon.

One afternoon a few weeks later, I arrived home from Golden Gate Park to find the kitchen wall a different shade of green. The air smelled like eucalyptus leaves.

Zach swore he'd done nothing. He stood up, stared at the wall. "I can't really see a difference, hon. Are you sure you're okay?"

"Of course I am. You just have to examine it very, very closely."

He smiled, looking unconvinced, and hugged me.

I painted the wall saffron yellow, a color Zach and I liked much better. Then I kept painting, filled with an intense energy. Using the oil-pastels my mother had left, I drew a woman, filled in a chalk-white face and a cap of dark curls. I gave her a swinging black cane. Not my mother. A mime. Her mouth was long and thin and vermillion-colored. I'd forgotten how much I loved vermillion. Streaks of ochre and ebony appeared in the background. I looked at the painting and decided I could do better. I pulled out an old sketch and replaced the mime with an immense, burnt-umber German Shepherd. I set him playing with a stubby-legged red dachshund, both of them crouched down like *What's next?*, their dog lips grinning. I felt wonderful. But after a day or so, that painting didn't look right, either. I bought new oils, my own set, splattered the wall with thick strings of titanium white, ultramarine deep, and cadmium yellow, using my body freely, Jackson Pollock style. Still I wasn't satisfied. As soon the oil dried, I repainted everything a smooth saffron, right back where I'd started from.

Huge sighs filled the apartment, hers or mine I wasn't sure.

I stopped painting and took on more dogs, becoming an expert five-leash walker, someone who people either grinned big at or shied away from, depending on their canine affinities. I tacked up notices on the bulletin boards in dog parks and advertised in the *SF Weekly*. Calls poured in—Nonie's owner had posted glowing Yelp reviews—and ended up with more work than I could handle. What little my mother had left was gone, and I needed the money. But did I really want to be a professional dog walker? I quit dog walking and joined Zach at Sports Basement. The shift supervisor was a tall, grim man who docked my pay the first day for being five minutes late.

࿇

Early one Saturday night, Zach and I were relaxing on the couch after a long week. The popcorn was freshly popped and still warm. The opening credits of *Room 237* were scrolling down the screen. A dog started barking outside, a high, chihuahua yipping. I looked out the window and saw only my own face hanging in the dark. There came a push of cool air. When I looked back around at the room, my mother sat in our gray-flowered chair—the chair that had once been hers—her feet propped up on the matching ottoman. The smell of formaldehyde was strong.

My mother lit an Extra Long. She was wearing a short, white tennis dress and socks with pink pompoms that showed over the backs of her Nikes. She'd never played tennis as far as I knew. Her tanned calves sported muscles as big as softballs and her shoulders looked huge. They seemed to grow broader as I stared. This scared me.

"Mom," I said, acting as if nothing were wrong. "You've got to stop showing up out of the blue. I told you, I have a life."

My mother scooched back in the chair as if she wasn't going anywhere. "Emma, I've tried, but nothing's working. Now I'm going to do this." She placed the cigarette between her index finger and thumb and slowly buried its tip in her thigh without the slightest wince of pain. When her hand lifted away, the smooth flesh was cratered a bloodless cerulean blue. She calmly twisted the cigarette in another spot. Iridescent vermillion appeared. Other marks came: rose, mars orange, and cinnabar. The brilliant wells of color had the effect of a bizarre painting.

I was horrified, but transfixed. "Mom," I said. "Why are you doing this? Why?"

"What was that, sweetie?" Zach said. "Did you say something?"

"You see her, don't you? Please say yes."

Zach shook his head. "But I know you do. It's all right,

Emma. I believe you."

My mother smiled. "See. He's worried, too."

"No, I'm fine," I told them both. "Really."

The next morning I got the Hoover out and vacuumed every square inch of our apartment.

LIKE FAMILY

"Are you the mother?" the nurse asks, checking Nicky's chart. Not *his* mother, but *the* mother. As if I was a cow and Nicky a calf. As if she didn't have a clue. Last week, it was the lady at the frozen yogurt place, before that, the man behind us at Safeway. Everybody wants to know. Am I Nicky's real mother?

We couldn't look less alike. Nicky is hair's black and thick, his coloring what people call olive. My skin's the kind of bright white you can almost see through, blue veins showing at my temples and neck. My hair is a curly red filling up with gray. Nicky's fingers are beautiful and long—fingers that could never have sprouted from the O'Connor family tree. We've got thick things with wide nails. Drew Walsh, my ex, has them, too. We've been separated a couple of years, though nobody's in a big hurry for a divorce.

Nicky leans his ten-year-old body now away from the nurse and me, acting like he's not listening in a way that tells me he is. I know the question bothers him, too. So driving home from the doctor's office, I tell him. Again.

"Nicky, your mother, the one who lives in New York,

65

she wanted the best for you. She was all alone, working two jobs. She had nothing a baby needs. No time, no savings, no help." In the rear view mirror I see him staring out the window.

"Nicky," I say a little louder, "your other mother couldn't raise you. That's why she found me on the day you were born in Highland Hospital and asked me to be your mother."

He keeps staring.

The boy deserves a story. Like every other kid in the world, he needs to hear about the day he was born, how he made his way from one body to the next, his own. He should know he didn't just appear one day in the white bassinet, or magically walk out somehow of *Goodnight Moon.* That he has a mother. Okay, two mothers. I try not to make a big deal about it. One works in an Allstate office in Oakland and lives with him on 31st Street. The other? The other, I say, moved back to upstate New York near where she grew up.

These aren't lies. They're just stories.

When Nicky was little, I'd be reading and find myself looking up. He'd be standing in the corner of the living room, eyelashes dark against his face. I put my book down and he'd come squeeze into the easy chair next to me.

"Hi," he'd say, as if it was the brightest word in the world. Nicky doesn't talk much. But sometimes he used to surprise me, tell me that Mrs. Blake read them *Nate the Great* today, and who happens to be the new four-square champion in the whole second grade: him.

But lately he stays on the far side of room in those Nikes and spiked up hair. He's taller than both Drew and I were at ten and a half, and thin. This Nicky doesn't say a word. Still, his eyes are full of questions, questions he doesn't ask. So I make stuff up. Maybe he's hungry. Or worried. Or both? I fix him his favorite snack—what I hope is still his favorite—ants on a log: raisins crawling up a stick of celery filled with peanut butter. He puts himself in front of the TV. Nicky would watch TV all day if I let him—*Happy Endings, Modern Family*, as if they're giving him clues to the world.

This much I do know. The day after Nicky was born, his other mother walked out of the hospital "for a quick cigarette," and never came back. The nurses found a note next to the baby. One word, in black pen. *Sorry*— The handwriting was neat, the letters even and lined up. I wonder what she meant. Sorry for him? Me? Her own self?

The hospital social worker called us that same afternoon. We'd been on the county list for almost three years. Drew was forty-seven by that time, me, forty-two, and soon we'd be too old to qualify as parents. Our house sits right across from Highland Hospital: 1401 East 31st. The yellow one with white roses out front. We crossed the street and fifteen minutes later I was a mother.

The nurses buried me in stuff: blankets, bottles, booties. A case of formula yet to expire. They wouldn't tell us her name, but they did offer the note they'd found on the bed. And his newborn cap, of course. I took everything, overwhelmed.

Now I pull into our narrow driveway and Nicky jumps out and runs to the front door. He's in such a hurry these days, that boy. Ready to grow up. When Nicky's umbilical cord fell off, I saved it. His newborn hat, the pink and blue knit he was wearing that first day—I kept that too. I saved everything. The chewed-on sippy cups and milk-stained undershirts. His first and best teddy bear still leaking stuffing. He used to like these things, the history I made for him. Yesterday, I brought out everything again.

"Mom," Nicky sighed. "I've seen all that."

&

Maybe I should have left it alone. If Nicky isn't asking, why should I? That's what Cecilia at the office said. At lunch she told me I was just looking for trouble. But I've decided to move ahead. It wasn't just the funny look the nurse gave me the other day, all the questions strangers have been asking. It's all that, plus. Plus what? Nicky's different now. I don't want to lose him.

His birth certificate, the one they sent months and months after he was born, isn't real. Lists me and Drew as the parents, like there had been never anybody else. If I'm wondering about her, Nicky has got to be, too.

When he was three, he climbed up under my T-shirt. He didn't say anything, just stuck his head in, stretching the white cotton way out.

"What are you doing?" I asked.

"I want to get born out of you," he said from underneath.

I tried not to laugh. My flesh. My flab. I felt sad and happy at the same time. Happy he wanted this. Sad it'd never happened. Everything I feel is complicated.

The woman whose body gave me his—I want to meet her, is all. Maybe that will help me understand my son better. Besides, someday Nicky's going to want the truth, or need the truth for something medical. There are tons of agencies on the internet that will do the searching for you. For a price, of course, but most, not very much. The one I picked sent the results incredibly fast, so fast I was sure it was a scam. But everything matches up. Gender, date, location.

Nicky's mother's not in New York, I discovered. She lives near Clear Lake, just a couple of hours north of here. In a town called Nice, on El Camino Drive. Her name is Lynetta.

Lynetta N. Desilva.

This Saturday, I decide, I'm driving up.

☙

Drew shows up at six on Wednesday, pretending that he hasn't the foggiest it's close to dinnertime. I don't throw him out. There's plenty of rosemary chicken and creamer potatoes and French cut green beans to go around. I set a plate at his old spot at the table.

Drew doesn't come around much, but he does help out. Watches Nicky when I have to work late, takes him to ball games sometimes. Gives us money, but never enough. He's the closest thing to a father Nicky's got.

I lay down another fork, knife, and spoon at the kitchen table. When Nicky was a baby, Drew and I took him to Clear Lake. We stayed in a Linger Longer cottage so small you met yourself coming and going. The lake was a soupy green and lined with trailer parks. I remember a blue and silver trailer, a single-wide with wood piled under its broken steps, a dog chained in the front yard, barking. We drove by. Drew and I drove by everything then.

Nicky picks at his food, like always. When I offer him berry cobbler, he shakes his head no. Nods when I ask if he's okay. Well, I can't make whatever's inside him come out. Nicky will talk when he's ready. I let him be excused.

As I'm pouring the coffee, Drew starts up again. Yesterday he said I was crazy to try to find Nicky's mother.

"Casey," he says. "Don't tell me you're still thinking of going up there."

"I am. That boy's so quiet these days. It's like I don't know him. I'm sure he was listening the other day at the doctor's office. Not just the question about my being his mother. But how I couldn't update the family history because he doesn't have one. I didn't mean it like that. Like he's got no family."

"Could be worse," Drew says. "My dad never came home from the war."

"It's not the same. You have photos, memories your mother's told you."

"Casey, you may not like what you find. Why stir things up?"

"I'm not stirring anything up. I'm driving to Clear Lake, is all. Whatever happens happens. "

I've never told Drew about the blankness I feel under my ribs. For years, I tried to coax a baby from my body. Drew had swimmers all over the place. Me, they gave pills, shots, tests every morning to pull the darkness out. Suddenly Nicky showed up. Carrying him out of the hospital, I burst into the tears. The nurses followed me down the hall. "Is everything all right?" they said. "Can we help?" I told them I was crying from happiness, but that was only part true. I was in shock.

I look at Drew. Maybe I'm not going just for Nicky's sake, but mine, too. That woman's the reason I have a son. Her body gave me what my own couldn't. It binds us together.

"Casey, you got your beautiful boy," Drew goes on. "What more could you want?"

I don't let the words *faithful husband* fly out of my mouth. He's been living with that woman over on Lakeshore for almost six months now. Maybe she'll want a baby of her own.

"Lynetta gave us that beautiful boy," I tell him. "That makes her like family. I just want to meet her. At least be able to call up a face."

He frowns and tilts his chair back. "Nobody in my family would walk out and leave a little baby like that."

"Right. You were real good at sticking around."

"Give me a break, would you, Casey? For once in your sweet life."

"Well, I'm going."

Drew's on his feet now, ready to leave, when I see Nicky standing in the shadow of the kitchen door, listening.

Damn! The last thing I wanted was for him to find out like this. I was going to tell him. As soon as I knew something about her for sure.

"Nicky—" I reach my hand out.

He walks past me and sits at the table, his shoulders hiked up to his ears. I go to smooth the hair down, but stop myself. I'm too old for that, he'd tell me. And those shoulders look skitterish.

"You hear anything you want to talk about?" I ask.

"Don't go there, Casey," Drew says.

"Did my mother really walk out and leave me?"

"Nicky—" And the same dumb thing comes out. "She wanted the best for you." I take in a breath. "Nobody knows what happened. Not even the doctors and nurses."

Nicky starts rolling a ball back and forth on the table, the one with the green eyeball floating inside it.

After Drew moved out, the house felt too big. Silence fell down and coated everything white. Table legs, spoons, the television. All blank white. Then Nicky would wake up from his nap and the house was too small. The press-me-again Old McDonald and Little Lamb songs, the graham-cracker goo on the supposedly washable tablecloth, the socks whose mates had gone missing. I'd have to leave, take Nicky to the mall. Shop it out. Inside, I'd find myself scanning the crowd. Is that his other mother? That woman in cinnamon-colored slacks? Her hair is dark enough. Or the one with the long thin hands? Nicky smiled and waved at just about everybody.

The stories got born then. Well, not really stories. Pictures floating into my brain. I see chewed fingernails, black polish. The rest fills in like a dream. A girl walks back and forth in a room on the ninth floor at Highland Hospital. Maternity. She touches a wall, presses her long fingers into it. Leans her head forward. Her black hair's so short it sticks up from her head. Her clothes—black high tops, blue jeans tied together with a long piece of string, a man's extra-large white shirt—lie crumpled in the corner. Her belly's so big it pulls her across the room. There's shame in that body, the way she keeps her elbows close. Maybe she thought California would be easier. Laid back.

Nicky's mother sneaks a cigarette in the cramped hospital bathroom, flicks the butt in the bloody toilet water, but it won't flush down. Now the pain is bone crushing.

Finally, the nurse comes in. "You have to stop all this screaming," she warns. "I know it hurts, but you're upsetting the others." They give her something, then something else, and something else, and Nicky slowly burns his way down. When he's half out, he pushes his arms out wide, now there are no fleshy walls to hold him. His fingers spread. He cries. And cries. She hates how he cries.

❧

"You okay?" I ask Nicky.

He rolls the green eyeball away. "Yeah."

"Would you like to come up with me and meet her?"

"Don't ask him that," Drew says. "How's a ten-year-old boy supposed to answer that?"

The eyeball travels back and forth another time before Nicky speaks. "No."

"You sure?"

He nods.

"What do you think about my going?"

Nicky's dark eyes finally find mine. For a moment I see a boy who wants to be like every other kid. Watch TV, drink cocoa, have a family that no one questions. Maybe I should call the whole thing off.

"I like it," he says, his voice lifting a little.

❧

Crossing the Carquinez Bridge, I can't stop looking at the bay. Today the gray water is perfectly still, not a boat, not a wave. Is this what Lynetta sees when she drives by? In Vallejo, I pull off 101 and stop at VIP Florist. It was Drew's idea. When Nicky said he'd liked my going, Drew got so he didn't want me to fail.

"Call her," he said. "At least give the woman some warning."

"You don't know me," I said when I phoned, "but I'm the one who—" Then came a hard click.

The second time, it was worse. I'd hardly said the word Highland and she cut me off, her voice ugly in my ear.

"Don't call here again. Ever."

That voice is all up in my body now. It buzzed in my head all night, rolling me over and over in the sheets. The woman probably won't even open the door.

But this morning I realized I couldn't call it off. What would I tell Nicky? That his mother, the one who takes care of him every day, was too scared? Wouldn't even give it a try?

So—flowers. "Nobody'd slam the door in the face of somebody delivering a beautiful bouquet of flowers," Drew said. At VIP's, I pick out the biggest one I can find. Every-

73

thing bright pink. Mr. Vip waits on me himself—he's wearing a name tag on his lapel—and wants to make sure I know the name of each flower: gerbera daisies, miniature tulips, pink carnations, and sweet something or other. He wraps them in orange tissue and rings me up. The flowers fill the footwell of my Toyota, pink eyes vibrating in all directions.

North of Calistoga, Highway 29 rises into a bunch of hairpin curves with drop-offs so steep I don't want to look. Just drive, I tell myself. I flip through radio stations, getting nothing but static. Near the top of the hill, the white shoebox I have on the seat slides and spills.

Scattered on top of the flowers now are two of Nicky's school photos I brought to show Lynetta. There's the one from first grade where the camera caught him in a big grin, a gap where his front teeth used to be, and this fall's, where he barely smiled and his hair was all gelled. Lynetta's note's near them. I look at the dark spot on Nicky's baby hat. It's blood, I decided a long while ago. His or hers, it doesn't matter, because at that point they were pretty much the same.

At Middletown, the road flattens out and big oak trees draw up close. I wonder what Lynetta looked like at Nicky's age, before the teens hit. Tall, probably had all that black hair, too. Or maybe it was red, like mine. Well, probably not red. I wonder if she's got kids—other kids—and trikes and Sit 'n Spins and Hello Kitty shoes all over her front steps. Could be she's found herself a nice husband. That's why she didn't want to talk to me. I imagine them at the kitchen table, Nicky's mother in fuzzy slippers and a blue nightgown.

Nicky's mother—there's no good word for what she is. What I am. *Adoptive mother* makes it sound like Nicky is a dog or a cat and I could give him back. I would never do that. Never. Just plain *mother* doesn't cover it. Lots of people say *real mother.* I've always hated the word *birthmother.* All I have to do is look at Nicky and see she gave him way more than birth.

Clear Lake looms into view. Mount Konocti rises on the far shore like a sleeping woman with roughly combed long hair. The lake below is anything but clear. In the nineties, someone decided water lilies would be pretty and infected the whole lake with Hydrilla. The water's thick with the weed now. Slimy. Impossible to see your feet once you're in past your knees, I hear.

I drive north on 29, the road skirting the lake, feeling myself get nervous. Finally Nice appears. Like the lake, the town doesn't live up to its name. A boarded up Tastee-Freez, and the only restaurant, Ed's Easy Does It, looks more like a bar. On the far side of town, I see El Camino. The road climbs uphill, twisting all the way. At the Newlove Trailer Park, I slow down but that's not it. I'm sure I'm lost now. But at the top, the street ends in a bunch of townhouses and a sign with the right address.

This place *is* nice. White clapboard with blue trim, rose-colored azaleas everywhere. My heart starts going crazy. Leave, I say to myself. Go. Tell Nicky, *Honey, she wasn't home.* On top of everything, the numbers on these townhouses make no sense. The five hundreds sit next to the three hundreds with single digits stuck in between. Whoever dreamed this system up didn't have visitors in mind.

Finally I see the buildings are grouped A, B, C, D to whatever. I jump out of the car before my mind can play any more tricks. I can't let myself go back, disappoint Nicky. I hurry across bright green lawns, pass dumpsters and tomato-heavy gardens. Number 215899 El Camino turns out to be way over in G. Nicky's mother's porch light is still on, though it's almost noon. Her concrete steps are empty. When I ring the bell, a dog sticks his nose under the fence next door and barks.

The door opens. I take in a big breath, keeping the flowers right in front of my face. "For you," I say.

"Really?" Nicky's mother's voice sounds high and happy like his can get.

"I'd be glad to bring this in, if you'd like. It's pretty big."

"All right."

Only one strip of sun makes it through the shades and lights up the blue rug in her living room. In front of the plush sofa sits a coffee table neatly lined with *Sunset* and *Woman's Day*. Magazines I read too. Everything in Lynetta's house is blue: the rug, the sofa, even, strangely, a few magazine covers. No toys, just a long stretch of quiet room. Against the far wall, a fish tank glows. A big-eyed fish swims to the top of the water.

"Where would you like me to set these?"

Nicky's mother takes the flowers and suddenly her face is in front mine. She's smiling now and her mouth forms that same happy square that Nicky's does. The woman's olive-skinned and good looking. Thin, too. Stand Nicky next to her and you'd say she was his mother. She has his head of thick black hair, though silver's winning out on the left. Wrinkles show at the corners of her eyes. Nicky's mother is not young at all. She's middle-aged. Maybe even fifty-two, like me. Though fifty-two looks better on her. I smile back.

She picks through the bouquet with long fingers—his long fingers—searching for a card. "Who are these from?"

"Your son." Even though I'd practiced the two words in my head on the drive up here, they come out like I want to hurt her. I don't.

"I don't have a son."

I go to place the ten-year-old note in her hand, but it flutters to the floor.

She glares. "Who sent you?"

"Nobody. Me." Well, not just me, I think. Nicky.

Lynetta walks to the couch and falls heavily into it. She crosses her legs. "I don't have to talk to you, you know."

"Should I go back and tell him that?" That came out the way I meant it to. Firm, but not mean.

"Could we not do this? Please."

"Twenty minutes is all, I swear, Lynetta. For Nicky's sake."

"Who?" Her forehead wrinkles. "Oh."

"His whole name is Nicolas O'Connor Walsh. O'Connor for my side."

She leans back against the couch like, *Twenty minutes, no more.* I sit in the black leather chair alongside her, looking around. Nicky's mother has touched everything in this room. The arm of this chair. The couch cushion. The wood-paneled walls. I wonder about the invisibilities that bodies leave behind. Cells, things smaller than cells.

"I shouldn't be surprised. You did call, I guess. But I always thought that if anyone ever showed up, it'd be him. Not the mother." She shrugs her shoulders like Nicky does when he doesn't want to talk but will let you. Strange how he has her gestures, too. Nicky's mother is wearing blue linen shorts, crisply ironed. Her yellow blouse is linen, too, neatly tucked over a flat stomach. I have on my usual, baggy Capris and white flip-flops. Clothes I thought would seem friendly. Now I lay the April *Sunset* over my less-than-thin lap and hide my big feet.

I'd thought I'd start out with something easy. Like

"Where do you work?" or "Does it get real hot up here?" or say something about the price of gasoline. But the way she lifts her shoulders and sets them down again reminds me too much of Nicky. I skip all that.

"What were you like?"

"What was I like?" Nicky's mother looks at my thick fingers. "I don't understand."

"You know. At ten." My voice is nervous. "Nicky's age now."

"You want to know that? Really?" She laughs and her eyes light up. "Well, I really loved to—" She stops. "I was your typical girl, I guess. Dolls. Bicycles. Jump ropes."

"Were you quiet?"

"I talked."

"No, I mean—"

"I was a normal child, if that's what you're driving at. Perfectly normal. And I'm a normal woman, too. What I did was so not unusual. "

"I know. Of course."

A silence goes by as I try to figure out how to get the conversation going in a different direction. Maybe Lynetta will ask about Nicky, what he likes to do. The room stays quiet.

"Would you mind if I asked you something else?"

"Go ahead." She shrugs.

"Well, it's— it's about Nicky being born. What did he— you know, do?"

Maybe Nicky didn't cry at all. Didn't push his arms out, looking for something familiar to hold him. Maybe he stared out of two swollen eyes, his quiet emptying the room. Maybe his first breath was soft. Kittenish. I've imagined so many things. Here is the woman who can tell me.

Lynetta shakes her head. "You ask the strangest questions." She tilts back and looks up at the ceiling. "They put him on my chest right away. He was still covered with, you know, all those fluids. His blue eyes stared up at me, and before I knew it, he'd clamped down on my breast. Hard. Like he'd never let go. The nurses kept telling me was what a good little eater he was."

Lynetta's voice is flat, as if the story belongs to someone else. I want to tell her Nicky doesn't eat like that anymore. I have to beg food into that boy. And his eyes aren't blue anymore.

She sighs and evens out the magazines corners so they're perfectly lined up. In the silence, the fish tank bubbles away. "When are you going to get to the real question?" she asks.

"The real question?"

"Why I left."

"I was working up to that." I pull the Nicky's newborn hat out and place it gently in front of her. "I saved all Nicky's baby stuff. I want you to know that."

"Look, I don't have all day."

"All right. Why did you walk away?"

She reaches for the knit hat, puts it down. "Maybe I realized the baby wasn't going to bring him back."

"Your husband."

"No, no. Not my ex. Robert. We met before my divorce was finalized. I fell hard, harder than I should have. Robert was the comptroller at Community Hospital in Santa Rosa. He always said he wanted kids. When I first found out I was pregnant, he seemed happy."

She sighs, and her yellow blouse billows a little. I imagine Nicky growing under that stiff fabric. His soft not-yet bones bumping up against hers.

"But right before I was due, Robert moved out of the

apartment we'd rented. God knows where. Took every shoe, every book."

"Why?"

"You think I know? Why don't you go ask him yourself?"

Him. I never thought about Nicky having another father out there, someone else who took off. I imagine Robert's face, a face Nicky might have someday. Wide at the temples. Crinkly dark eyes. Nothing like Drew's. I see him packing a box, a frown coming onto his face.

"Don't look at me like that. I did what I had to. Highland Hospital was a place I knew no one would know me. Ask questions. When I got home, I told some story about the baby not making it. Everybody felt sorry for me, even my ex."

Sorry. That word.

She says, "I almost went back. It was lovely the day after he was born, clear and hot and blue, the way Oakland can get in September. Not a bit of fog. I'm not stupid, you know. I'd seen the signs. Highland Hospital was a safe surrender site. I knew people would line up for a healthy baby. You did."

"Don't you ever wonder about him?"

She focuses her brown eyes on mine. "I had no interest being a single mother. After he was born, I moved to Napa to manage a hotel. Five years ago, I came up here to oversee another. I like living alone. I do. I can cook. Not cook. Read all night. Sleep in. Like this morning. Nobody bothers me. "

Maybe if she sees what he looks like, I think, she'll be interested.

"He's a great kid, Nicky." I set the school photos side by side on her coffee table. "This is him in first grade, right after he lost both front teeth. And here he is this fall."

She looks at both photos blankly. "He's a cute boy. You

must be doing a good job."

Her compliment comes way too easily. Like if she says something nice, maybe I'll clear out. I feel Nicky's mother leaving him, leaving us, all over again. Something in me rises to the surface, something impatient and smooth and hungry.

"Why can't you say his name, Lynetta? Nicky."

"Nicky. Nicky! Happy now?" She sighs.

It's like air being let out of a balloon. Everything around me turns silent, ordinary, and blue. The woman couldn't care less about Nicky. And his father—Robert—couldn't be bothered either. I lay my head back and leave it there. The big-eyed fish swims to the corner of the tank and stares.

"I should have told you," she says. "I go by Nadine now, my middle name."

The fins flutter.

"I guess this isn't what you wanted to hear."

"It's okay."

"Well, you were the one who decided to come." She slides the baby hat across the coffee table.

"What should I say to Nicky?"

"Tell him whatever you want," she says. "Whatever he needs. You're his mother."

"And what are you?"

"What I did is done." She stands and looks down at me. "Listen, if it helps, feel free to go ahead and act as if."

"As if? What's that mean?"

"Pretend. Act as if I don't exist. I can't do either of you any good now." She smiles for a moment and walks to front door.

I want to say something before I leave. Tell her I'm sorry things turned out the way they did and that guy's a jerk, and

I'm so glad she brought Nicky into the world. My world.

"Good-bye" is all I say.

At the bottom of the hill, I drive straight ahead instead of turning onto the highway. Somebody told me that Clear Lake got so low once that you could walk all the way across. At the foot of Mountain Konocti, a cave appeared, then a cavern, then a hidden lake. Not as big as Clear Lake, but still big. Something you'd miss if you didn't know where to look. The creatures inside were all bright white, their eyes pink and blind. Some had no eyes at all.

I pull up in front of a covered walkway that leads to the water. It's pretty, lined with hanging baskets of yellow geraniums. I sit there looking at the murky water and finally get out of the car. The sun is directly overhead now, and hot. I can feel it burning my hair. I remember that feeling as a child, hair so hot it felt red. Which it was. Gray's not all that different. My feet move me towards the lake. The sand is a pure white that must have been put there for tourists. In my flip-flops, I feel its cool, then cold underlayer.

HERE I AM

I'm the last thing people imagine when they think of a funeral director. For this late night house call, I'm wearing a purple dress and heels to match; my nails are painted lavender. I'm hardly the dowdy thing in black the family expected.

The son hesitates, but shows me in. First, I verify that their grandmother is in fact dead: breath and pulse, no, and doll's eye test, negative. The old woman's eyes roll right along with her head. Though the hospice doctor's been here and gone, you can't be too careful in this business. Last week, some guy in Mississippi woke up in a body bag on the embalming table. It was all over the news.

I sit down with a few family members, who want to talk funeral arrangements. "I'd be glad to answer all your questions," I say. "Or I could come back tomorrow, if that's easier." No, they just want everything over with. I open the brochure, we discuss options, and I tell them about my special.

"For nineteen hundred and ninety-nine dollars," I say, "you get a one-day funeral, including a premier velvet-lined mahogany casket for the viewing, all the embalming, cosmetology, dressing, and supervision, two silk flower arrangements, and the use of my S&S superior hearse." After that, the body is buried in cardboard. Thick, ecological cardboard. A lot of people like that. They did.

I cocoon the grandmother in the flowered bed sheet, line the gurney up with the mattress, and start to slide her heavy body. It doesn't budge. This has never happened to me before, not with family present.

"Here," the son says. "Let me help."

"No, thank you," I say in what I hope is a professional voice. The last thing I want is for him to help me. But I can't just yank or shove. The old woman deserves respect. The breath feels stuck in my throat. Finally, slowly, I check the sheet and pull it from where it's wedged between the bed and gurney. Of course. Now the grandmother's shoulders slide, then her fleshy legs. When the body's firmly on the gurney, I strap her in.

"Sometimes it takes a bit of doing," I tell the son.

He nods.

In the last fourteen hours, I've arranged three funerals, made two house calls, set up chairs for a wake and broken them down again, ordered flowers, and filed out more forms with the City and County of San Francisco than I want to think about.

Exhausted, I ride the elevator down to my hearse parked in the basement and drive out into the October rain. North Beach is quiet this time of night. After dropping the body off at my embalmers', I head back to the office. There's still work to do.

When the doorbell rings, I have to pick my head up from my desk. It buzzes again. I groggily check in the mirror, wipe away the mascara raccooned under my eyes, and straighten my stockings. I live right upstairs from the funeral parlor. People call at all hours.

"Lena," a man's voice says.

In the window near the door, all I see is a hat, a stiff gray dome with a red-tipped black feather. I don't know anyone with a hat like that.

"Lena," he calls again.

"Denis?" I say, opening the door. "I don't believe it." We dated a couple years back. Not serious but not *not* serious either. After my divorce, I swore I'd keep it causal with men.

Denis's face looks broad and smooth; only a few silvery strands show in his hair. He combs it back now, which makes him look more like the financial adviser that he is—or was. We haven't been in touch. He's got the same strong forearms and muscular legs of an athlete that I remember loving. But his eyes, a sapphire blue, are sad in a way I'd never seen.

"Well, hi," I say.

"You look good, Lena," he says, taking in my silky dress and high heels. "Wow." He pauses and moves his eyes away. "Look, I'm sorry. It's late, I know. I—it's my mother, Lena. She's not well. The doctor told me tonight that she may not have much longer. Mom's always said she wants you to handle her funeral when the time comes. I thought you should know."

I met Denis's mother at a viewing. I remember her as small, lively woman with a gigantic smile. His mother was the one introduced us.

He could have called, of course. But that thought doesn't stay in my head because the rain that's turned to mist is glistening now along Denis's broad shoulders. I reach out and touch his fingers on the door. He doesn't pull away.

Denis and I dated maybe five or six months. He was surprised by my profession but not in the least put off. Me, I wanted a fling. I talked him into heading across the bridge to Berkeley for a little Zydeco dancing, and he took me to that restaurant in Chinatown where the waiters are so rude all you can do is laugh. I liked to show up sometimes at his door wearing sequins, a white stole, and tiara. He didn't dress up, but he sure liked how I looked. We took selfies: I'd glam it up and he'd keep his face drawn and serious, or he'd be the big black-suited man with me just in his shadow.

One Friday night, Denis suggested we go for a drink at the Tonga Room in the Fairmount hotel.

"You've put in a long week," he said. "Let's relax." Except he was nervous, fussing with his collar stays and dropping nickels and dimes all over the floor. I leaned back and ordered a Mai Tai, trying not to notice. We watched the Tonga's thunderstorm show, lightning flashing when you least expect it. Afterward, Denis cleared his throat.

"Lena," he began. "Why—What would you say to our moving in together? Plenty of room at my house. You're always saying how much you love the view of the Golden Gate."

My head jerked back, I was that surprised. My divorce had hit hard. I had bought the funeral parlor with my ex and assumed it was for life. My mind went to other men— all the husbands, brothers, fathers—whose bodies I'd bent over, there one day and suddenly no more. My heart began to pound.

"Denis," I managed. "You know I can't just move my business across town."

He nodded and took a sip of water. We talked of other

things. But hell if I know what because all I can remember now is Denis's hollow-eyed look of pain.

We never saw each other again. No big blow up, no bitter words. Denis would phone from time to time, and I'd call back. Until about a year ago. I don't know why. I kept meaning to.

"Of course," I say now. "I'd be honored to take care of the arrangements." Ignoring how late it is, I add, "Why don't you come in?"

After things ended with Denis, I threw myself into work. I found comfort in its routine, the perfect positioning of flowers, the right combination of songs to honor a life. Putting on a funeral is a huge production, more complicated than a wedding. I'm creating final memories that people will never forget. And I have just one shot to get it right.

Of course, I've had a few, what? one-night stands—the guy from the espresso place, the salesman who kept me in guest registries, a married neighbor. But none of these men made me feel the way Denis did—as if I were the only woman in the world.

I usher him into the softly lit foyer. I've made the place look like a home, with thick oriental rugs and a long couch that a body—two bodies?—could sink into without a second thought. He glances around uncomfortably. I walk him to the office. It's filled now with fresh flowers: pumpkin-colored mums, pale lilies, and immense ferns, moist and sweet-smelling.

Denis takes the chair next to mine. He nervously taps his finger on the glass desktop.

"I'm sorry," I say. "Where are my manners? Beer? Wine? I have both." I pull out two tall glasses from the stocked refrigerator behind the desk and set them in front of us.

He quickly shakes his head. His mother, he says, wants a simple service, the music lively—you know how she loves a good party, Lena—and the food plentiful. Antipasti, ravioli, and cannoli—chocolate and vanilla—from Stella Pastry. He talks faster and faster, looking at me less and less. The desire I'd just felt—I'm sure he felt it, too—begins to evaporate.

The grandmother I'd collected in North Beach comes back to me the next day. They've sutured her mouth shut from the inside and plumped her eyelids with caps so they'll maintain a natural shape. Her skin is firm, and her body, if anything, heavier from the embalming fluids. Getting on the maroon pantsuit that the family wants to see her in should be about as easy as putting a party dress on a pine tree. I lift one thick leg, and tug the pants up, trying not to rip the fabric. The other leg goes even slower. Finally I ease the pants over her hips. Threading the fabric belt around her waist is easy.

A deep quiet envelopes us as I turn to her makeup. I color her lips rose and the eyelids sable brown. I use regular makeup, not the heavy mortuary kind, because it's natural. I want her to look sleeping, not dead. I blue her hair—just a bit—to brighten its gray under the lights, and tilt her chin down for a peaceful look. The work absorbs me, makes me forget about Denis.

A week later, I'm downstairs getting ready for the party. Fifteen years ago—right after I bought the business from my ex—I threw my first Halloween bash. Now, it's an annual thing. Put a bunch of San Franciscans in costumes and something interesting always happens.

Denis phoned yesterday to tell me his mother was doing

better, still in the hospital but hanging on, at least for now. I invited him to the party.

"Come. You can get out for a couple hours and have fun. Your mother would tell you the same thing."

Denis said he'd try to swing by. Last Halloween I surprised everyone by popping out of a coffin in a leopard miniskirt at midnight. This year I planned to top that.

I lay a tuxedo-clad Dracula in a coffin and convert a child's casket into the beer cooler. For a couch, I pull out the longest coffin I have, fit milk crates inside, and stack sofa pillows on top. Tiny ghoul lights with feathery eyes get sprinkled around. The band, Mechanical Heart, arrives and starts to set up.

At nine, the party is coming alive. Marie, my neighbor and part-time bookkeeper, shows up as Marilyn, with more voluptuous cleavage than the star ever had in real life. Her caveman husband wears a cowhide slung over his shoulder and a bone stuck through his ponytail. This leads to predictable jokes about boners. It's true, I tell them, the dead do get them. Everybody laughs and shots of tequila go around.

The band is deep into their second set—Derek and the Dominos, The Dead, U2—playing so hard that people can't help but dance. I replenish the cocktail hot dogs and refill the Skittles bowl, and finally get out there myself. I dance with a handsome skeleton, adding a little shimmy here and there, but my usual verve's missing. Where is Denis?

At eleven forty-five, I signal the band, and Marie and I sneak upstairs. It was her idea—the low-cut black leather vest and micro skirt, the studded boots—she discovered the whole outfit in Fantasy on Folsom. All I did was add the whip. I can't wait to see Denis's face.

Marie laces me in and zips me up. We tiptoe down the backstairs and I tuck myself into the casket we'd propped up on wheels. She rolls me toward the band, who've begun a loud countdown. At exactly midnight, I jump out.

"Can't get no satisfaction—" I sing. The last syllable comes out like a low growl and everybody cheers. *"'Cause I try and I try and I try—"*

Under the lights, I suddenly feel everyone's eyes on me, and, as if someone threw a switch, my confidence disappears. Here I am surrounded by friends, but now I feel as if none of them knows me: the exhausted me, the lonely me. I scan the crowd for Denis. He's not here. I go to sing the next word, but nothing comes out. Now people are staring.

A guy tosses a handful of candy corn up in the air. Someone else throws M&M's. Everything starts zinging—bits of orange, blue, yellow flying past. A gangly orangutan catches Kit Kats in his hairy palms. A French maid holds out her gauze skirt for Starbursts. People laugh.

They think it's part of the act. The switch flips back on and I snap my whip high over everyone's heads. They scream and applaud. I grab a fistful of candy from the stage and pitch it back out at the crowd.

That's when I see Denis, standing uncomfortably alone in the back. He's wearing a retro bowling shirt with ANTONY stitched over the pocket, patched Madras shorts, and sloppy brown sandals, something that doesn't look like a costume, but is. Denis is an impeccable dresser, tailored suits, polished wingtips, vests. I've always liked that about him. But you know, tonight the shorts look good on him. I flash a smile.

Denis doesn't smile back. He isn't scooping up candy and tossing it. He just stands there awkwardly, his legs planted stiffly under him. I finish the song and make my way back.

"Hi," I said, still out of breath. "You made it. Great."

"Hello." Denis's eyes move to my leather vest.

"How is your mother?"

"Fine." That word comes out like the first, clipped. His gaze lowers to my boots.

"Is everything okay?"

"Yes," he lies. Because when he looks up, I see the same expression of pain he had after asking me to move in. "Do you mind my asking, Lena? Is that supposed to be a costume?"

"Sure," I say, surprised. Could Denis have become strait-laced? Or be jealous? I'd only ever dressed up for him. I continue as if nothing's wrong. "You know Fantasy over on Folsom? Well Marie—"

Somebody shouts "Lena!" above the roar of the party. I spin around. The married guy down the street—whatever we had is long over—shoots me a big grin.

Denis frowns. "I've got to go, Lena," he says. "I've an early meeting tomorrow morning.

"You were terrific!" my neighbor yells, lifting his beer. I wave and smile back. When I turn around, Denis isn't there.

☙

After the nurse wheels the empty IV pole out of the room, I stare down at Denis's mother's body. She has this strange half-smile on her face, her mouth slightly open as if she wants me to lean closer, tell me a joke, or some secret about the afterlife. After all these years in this business, of course I have opinions. What waits for us is not heaven or hell, but infinite blank space, a stretching soft nothingness. But maybe I'm wrong. Maybe we all are.

So why not? I put my ear near Denis's mother's mouth, wondering what I'll hear. Nothing. Just an all-too-familiar silence.

Then I do hear something, a sound I don't recognize at first. It comes again. My own breath. I feel air sliding down my throat, filling my ribs. It feels good, all this air.

Denis's mother died a week and a half after the party, her eyes open until the last day and then seeming to rally at the very end. Denis called to tell me at four in morning.

"It's late," he said. "I'm sorry. My timing's always off." His voice dropped.

"Stop, will you. This is what I do." Even in these circumstances, it was good to hear his voice. "How are you, Denis?"

"About the arrangements," he continued as if he hadn't heard. "Let's go with what we discussed. A short service, upbeat music, lots of food. You know my mother." Then he wanted off the phone.

She's so light, Denis's mother, so easy to lift from the hospital bed, her legs and arms neatly folding in. I drive the hearse through the gray first light of morning to the embalmers. Forty-eight hours later, she returns to me, pinker and firm. The pleated, sparkling dress that Denis dropped off in my absence slips on without a struggle. I tuck the shimmering fabric around the edges of her thin body and gently spray her white, white hair. I lift the half-smile back on her face. She looks the way I want her to, a mysterious sad-happy.

The wake isn't crowded. At eighty-three, Denis's mother has outlived most of her friends. A few cousins—I think they're cousins—stroll in early and gather around the casket. I had expected Denis to arrive early and want to go over everything, but he shows up right before the service. He nods briefly at me and stays near the door, shaking people's hands. They trickle in, one or two at a time, but enough to keep him there.

I busy myself making sure the candles stay lit and picking up a stray flower petal here and there. "The energy that woman had," I hear someone say. "Every morning, a huge breakfast, fried eggs, pancakes. Maybe that was her secret." What secret, he doesn't say. Conversation continues to swirl around me. Finally the minister goes to the lectern and everyone sits. After an hour or so, things start winding down and Denis goes back to the door. I walk over.

"I'm sorry," I say. "Your mother was a fine woman."

"Thank you." His eyes veer away. "She lived a long life. It was time."

The room fills with music from the speakers overhead, a jazzy version of "Anything Goes" that I'd picked out.

"I want you to know," I say, "I do something crazy every year. For Halloween."

"You want to talk about this now?" Denis whispers, looking over his shoulder.

"Well—yes. For a moment. You've been avoiding me."

"All right," he says, sucking in a breath. "I'll tell you. Lena, I was embarrassed. For you more than me. I mean, the comments. This guy kept saying, Is that hot or what. Then somebody else started in with the hand motions. And that man yelling. I'm sorry, I just had to leave."

I can't help but grin. So he was jealous. But if I couldn't go a little wild in midlife, then when could I?

"Oh those guys," I say, touching his fingers. "They didn't mean anything. I know them. They come every year."

"I'll bet," he says loudly.

A woman reaches out a delicate hand with neat, unpolished nails. She leans close to Denis and their shoulders touch. "Hello," she says, looking right at me.

Her ash-colored hair—neither blonde nor brown—is perfectly coiffed. This woman in a black dress with a silver ballerina pinned to the collar has been standing next to Denis this entire time, except I never saw her. It never crossed my busy mind that Denis might come with another woman.

Her cheekbones are high and faintly rouged. "You must be Lena Vincent," she says. "I've heard so much about you. Everything looks lovely. Just the way Mrs. Clark would have wanted it."

"So what did you say back?" Marie asks me the next day. All morning I'd circled my apartment in sweats and bare feet, trying to stop thinking about that woman. Finally I combed my hair, put on a decent dress, and went downstairs. The next thing I knew I was fiddling with the foyer lights. I couldn't stop moving, fixing, arranging. Finally I phoned Marie and asked if I could drop off some receipts for her to tally.

"Of course," she'd said. "Stay for coffee." Now we're sitting by her kitchen window overlooking Washington Square Park. Benjamin Franklin's metallic head glitters in the sun.

"Oh, I just mumbled something. And walked away."

"You mumbled? I've never heard you do anything close to mumble."

"That woman intimidated me. Her appropriately black dress. The way she'd removed polish from her nails. You could still see a little around the cuticles. I never take the polish off my nails. In fact, for a wake, I brighten it." I spread my fingers on top of the table so Marie could see. Fiesta, a brilliant coral I've been wearing for years.

Marie pours me another cup of coffee and pushes the creamer closer. "Lena, I can't say as I blame the man. First you don't want him. Then you do. Does he even know how

94

you feel? Denis always struck me as a nice guy. What happened?"

"What happened? We had fun. He was nice. Oh—I don't know. His teeth, maybe. You could see spinach stuck in them sometimes."

"You're kidding me. You ditched Denis because he had spinach in his teeth? You who likes to live life big?"

That stops me. I didn't think of myself as living big, but just flat-out living. Having the best time with what time I had. My eyes squeeze together.

Something had scared me about Denis, something I sensed before but now hits me full on. Yes, there was the problem of how I'd handle my business if I moved in with Denis, but we could have worked that out. The thing was— sex. Okay, more than sex, but that's what got it started.

One night, we were sitting on Denis's cut-velvet couch drinking a little Chivas, and we ended up in his big bedroom. It was May, warm, and all the windows open. Denis's white cat lay on his Persian rug. We sprawled out naked on the bed. Denis slowly kissed my neck, the tip of my collarbone and shoulder, then my lips, big open-mouth kisses that sent sparks down my veins. I felt his body against mine, immense and silky. I didn't want to stop. Not this, not him, not us. The cat jumped on the bed and batted at something on the window screen and still we didn't stop.

When the sun broke through the next morning, it woke me from a good, hard sleep. I heard Denis downstairs, the sound of coffee brewing and spoons clinking. Breakfast smells came. Before I knew it, I was huddled in Denis's bathroom, setting off my own ringtone, and saying loudly, "Yes, of course. I'll be right there."

It scared the hell out of me, wanting Denis like that. I

must have walked myself around my car three times before I drove off to work. The next week, Denis asked me to move in.

∾

I hand the expenses from Denis's mother's funeral to Marie to process. When she gives me back the bill to sign, I wonder if I should add a note at the top. But what? Dear Denis, Hey D, Thinking of you..., something else entirely? Finally I settle on a neutral, Thanks. Call anytime with questions, and sign it with a flourishy L.

Days go by. Through my office window, I hear people walking outside, their shoes sound heavy: boots, lace-ups. North Beach is busy this time of year. Voices talk about gravy recipes and what pound turkey to buy. It's almost Thanksgiving, everyone's getting ready for family and friends to arrive. Marie has invited me to eat with them again this year. I told her I'd try. The holidays are my busiest time. Deaths keep building from Thanksgiving to New Year's. Christmas Day, in fact, is often the worst. Nobody knows why, not even the experts. My personal theory is holiday stress. High expectations and no downtime.

In the afternoon I'm talking with a couple who have an uncle in hospice. The phone rings and I let the call click over to voicemail. Money's no object with these people and we've lots to decide. When I finally get a chance to check the messages, I hear Denis's voice.

"Hello Lena," he says. Then he goes silent as if I'm about to pick up. "I got your bill," he finally continues. "It doesn't seem right to just mail you a check. The funeral was—" Another pause, shorter than the first. "Stunning." I've never heard Denis use that word before.

"How about I stop by?" he says. "I mean, if you're not

too busy." Another pause. "This is Denis. You've probably guessed that. I just wanted to—make sure. Call me, okay? Bye. Either way. Okay? Bye."

I don't phone Denis right away. It's not just that word—stunning—that has me wondering. It's his whole voice. Faster, and more energetic. He certainly isn't going to ask me to move in again. Sex? Is that what he's after? I've seen grief do that to people, wear away a layer of formality. Drive them into other people's arms.

"Sure. Come by," I tell him later, trying to sound casual, which is much easier over the phone. We bat around times and end up with Saturday morning.

"I have two funerals later," I say. "But nine o'clock should be fine."

"Terrific," Denis says in that new voice of his.

Saturday morning, I'm up before seven fussing with my hair. My bangs stick together and the whole left side won't lie straight. And I can't decide what to wear. Finally I pick out a robin's egg blue A-line, something more traditional than usual, but that still shows off my legs. I add a strand of silvery pearls.

I walk into the mortuary. At ten thirty this morning, we have Dr. Guffano, a surgeon who had a thriving practice in North Beach for forty-odd years, someone I've heard of but never met. He's a narrow-chinned man with arms that rest peacefully inside the casket. Someone with a re-markably unwrinkled face that doesn't need much. A little powder, pink blusher, tawny lipstick, that's it. I trim a few nose hairs, smooth an eyebrow, and straighten his striped tie. I move the wreath near the casket to make more room for the flowers Dr. Guffano's widow had me special order. But the Stargazer lilies and orange chrysanthemums haven't arrived yet. The doctor has a big family coming, a loving family, who want to honor a life well lived.

Nine o'clock comes and goes. Nine-thirty. I pick a speck of lint off the coffin, tilt the lid open a fraction more. Just stopping by, I think. Dropping off a check. What kind of life have I lived? I stare at an empty chair. I want to dive back into bed, blot out the morning.

No chance of that. The wreath is still missing. And that's what the widow will look for first thing when she walks through the door.

"You're kidding," I say to Ramon at the Secret Garden when he tells me the arrangement isn't quite finished yet. After all the business I've thrown their way.

"Please see that the wreath is ready," I tell him. "I'm coming right over." I can drive there faster than they'll be able to deliver them.

I phone Marie and see if she can hold down the fort. Just a few minutes, I tell her, so I can get to the flower place on Columbus and back. Sure, she says. She's done this before. I take my Cadillac hearse. No one dares ticket a hearse.

But Columbus Avenue is jammed, and the side streets, worse. All of San Francisco is out, people streaming by holding pie-shaped boxes, or trying to balance two, three shopping bags. A Porsche, SUV, and Chevy pickup fight for the only parking space in sight and a Mercedes sits on the sidewalk in front of Peet's Coffee, its emergency lights flashing. Pedestrians weave in and out of the traffic, not even bothering to make it to the crosswalk.

As I inch by, people stare at the silver hearse. The morning started out cool and gray—cold, really—but now it's warm, a Bay Area Thanksgiving warm. I roll down the window, roll it up again. The brake lights ahead stay red, a horn blares. Shit. Forty-five minutes until Dr. Guffano's funeral. "I haven't even hit Jackson Street yet," I say when I phone Marie. "Can you greet any early birds?" She agrees. The light turns red, green, and red again.

My phone rings. A second later, I hear pounding on the back of the hearse. What the hell? I answer the phone and suddenly there is Denis standing outside my door. He taps on the window, his cell pressed to his head.

"Lena," he says in my ear. "Could you please let me in? Marie said you were stuck in traffic."

"What happened?" I say, opening the window. We put our phones down. "You weren't there."

"Yes, I—"

A horn blasts.

"You'd better get in." I click open the passenger door.

Denis settles in the seat, blinking, and looking around the dark interior. "I've never been the inside one of these before. It's huge. Curtains and everything." He turns and stares through the sheer cotton panels into the empty space behind us.

I stare at his legs. He's wearing shorts, not Madras, but smooth beige khakis, and the loose brown sandals I remember from the party. I couldn't see his legs that night—too crowded—but now his calves look strangely familiar. They're covered lightly with dark hair, which emphasizes his almost-delicate looking ankles.

"What happened? Tell me."

"Lena, I was there. Ten. Right on the dot."

"Denis, we agreed on nine o'clock. Remember?"

"No. It was definitely ten." Sweat is starting to bead on Denis' forehead. He smooths his hair with the flat of his hand. "Oh—it doesn't matter. Here I am. Here you are. We made it." His dark blue eyes flash.

"Right," I say, irritated. "Great morning. No flowers. Terrible traffic. You."

Denis stretches out a long leg. "So," he says, ignoring what I just said. "I wanted to thank you, Lena. You know, in person. You did a wonderful job with the funeral. Everything was stunning." There's that word again, as if he practiced it, as if he practiced all these words.

"You're welcome," I say. "Your mother was a good woman." All this urgency for a thank you? But we talk on— Thanksgiving, the warm weather—until abruptly Denis is silent.

"You're probably wondering," he finally says.

This time I don't hold back. "You're right. Who is she?"

"She?"

"The woman at the funeral."

"Alta, you mean? A friend."

"I'll bet," I say. My reflection crawls by in an empty bookstore window— my head looks warped in the glass, one silver pearl is stretched big. "Denis, I know you've moved on. It's really none of my business."

"That's the whole point. I—I haven't moved on. " He talks quickly now. How, okay, Alta was a girlfriend, of sorts, but that's over now. He dated other women, too, over the past couple years, but nothing worked out. None of them were any fun. He looks right at me. "Then my mother—"

"I know." I slide my foot off the brake and the hearse slips forward. "I really am sorry."

"No—I mean, thank you. I miss her, all the time. You two were alike, I think. More than I realized. But that's not what I wanted to say." He pulls in a shaky breath. "When I asked you to move in, Lena, suddenly like that, I knew it was wrong from the second I saw your eyes change. We could have kept going. I mean, the—everything was amazing. But I couldn't take the words back, could I? Not without making everything much worse."

My mind zings back and forth: Dr. Guffano's widow probably walking through the door this very minute, the gap where her flowers are supposed to be, what Denis really means.

"I blew it, Lena."

In the silence that follows, a strange suspended moment holds me. The brake lights blur ahead but I barely see them.

It's this moment that I would remember decades later, after our long marriage, and Denis's death, which was not sudden but lingering, full of remissions and on-and-off hope. How still and blue his eyes look now, unblinking now as they would be later when I'd bend over his body, tears staining his pink cheeks. Because I'd dress Denis, too, put him in a soft green shirt open at the collar and slip brown sandals on his feet, the sandals he'd worn to the party, is wearing today. No one would know they were there but me.

Denis lets out a long, half-whistle of a breath. "Guess I just blew it again." He reaches for the door handle.

"No. It wasn't just you." When he looks confused, I finally admit, "Who made mistakes."

Denis smiles a small—infuriatingly small—smile. He catches my fingers in his. Now he's taking my hand, arm, shoulder, and pulling me close. Kissing me. His mouth tastes like some kind of sweet-salty spice and his sweaty smell, I love it.

Horns shriek. The flowers! I quickly drive forward to fill the gap that's opened ahead of us. But the traffic refuses to let up. Maybe Denis and I should get out, walk. The flower shop's not far. Maybe we could make it there faster than driving. I imagine petals, moist coolness, dark green.

But I can't just leave the hearse.

"What are you doing?" Denis says when I suddenly veer toward the sidewalk.

People part like we're a silver tidal wave coming. A few don't look surprised. This is San Francisco. I slowly edge the tires up and over the curb. But as soon as we've cleared the concrete, I stop and gun the engine of the hearse. Just for the hell of it.

BREATHE

Lewis had been wanting some of that nitrous for hours. He'd had this dream—a predawn dream—that must have had something to do with his father dying because he couldn't get the hospital stink out of his head. He'd woken up with his jaw burning, a back tooth singing out with pain.

He had switched years ago from a perfectly fine dentist over on Divisadero to Ed Karr here in Noe Valley because Karr had nitrous. The drywall guy Lewis had been working with at the time swore by it. "Nitrous messes with your head in the best possible way," he'd grinned. Said Karr was pretty free with the stuff. Free was right. Floating free, his head plastered against the ceiling, his body drifting below, Karr's beige walls tingling.

"The doctor will be right in," a voice called. He caught sight of the blonde woman who had shown him the room and disappeared. A new dental assistant, Lewis supposed. She hadn't been here three months ago.

He flipped through the *National Geographic* she'd handed him to read, planets colliding on the cover, orange and purples erupting. He pulled up one sock and bunched it down tightly again. Four Advil had only kicked back the pain some. Where was old Karr?

Outside, branches with hanging green things pushed against Karr's picture window as if they wanted in. Wild fruit maybe. Lewis closed his eyes, reopened them. Helena would know. His wife must have spent half of the twenty-seven years they'd been married in the backyard tending one thing or another. San Francisco's amazing, she said. Green even in winter. Helena knew the names of living things. He knew about houses, built dozens. Knew how to get a frame up quickly in the rain, hang a door so it closed with a satisfying click, slam in one nail after the other.

Karr walked into the room. "Lew," he said, "How's it going?"

Lewis lifted himself off the chair enough to shake Karr's hand. "Not bad, Ed." His dentist's palm felt moist as always, spongy.

Karr sat and swiveled the stool closer. His hair lifted in gelled strands that swept across his head in a buoyant curve. "Nice win for the Warriors yesterday. Did you catch the game?"

"Nah. I had to work. It's busy."

"That's a good thing in construction, right? Busy?"

"Right." Lewis stared out the window.

"So. Your tooth." Karr flipped on the dental light and Lewis opened his mouth. He felt a stab of pain.

"Crown, definitely," Karr said, glancing at the chart. "Looks like bruxism might be a factor. Are you having trouble sleeping, Lew? Any jaw pain?"

Lewis folded his hands tightly over his chest. "No."

Fuck if he was going to say anything. He'd started grinding his teeth six months ago after his father was admitted

104

to the ICU and it'd gotten worse since. Whole days went by he could hardly chew. Karr wasn't the only one who wanted to know what was wrong, or in Helena's case, why he was so sad, so angry. In the beginning, he'd blurt out his father had just died. *Sorry,* they'd say. *I'm so sorry for your loss.* Helen looked at him with sad eyes. Well, the last thing he wanted was Karr's pity.

A few months ago, he was pedaling through Golden Gate Park, looked over, and saw Karr riding next to him. "Gorgeous day," Karr had said, slowing down. But even that had been too fast. Lewis sucked in his breath so it wouldn't sound like it was coming hard, was able to shoot the breeze—for a second—until Karr passed, and waving, rode out of sight. Down by the windmill, there was his dentist again. Waiting for him, it seemed. Christ. What could Lewis do but try to ride alongside? Get winded all over again.

An invitation had come. Beer at Karr's place, which turned out to be a condo on Nob Hill with two bridge views. He and Helena lived on a narrow street in Bernal Heights near 280. After a few Jolly Pumpkins, Karr showed Lewis the training bike he'd set up in front of the big screen, the custom Fuji-Sportif for zipping across the Golden Gate, the mountain bike he used to climb up and over Mount Tam. Twice in a day. In the spare bedroom, Karr had stashed Speedplay cyclers, portable tool kits, screw-in spike cleats for the occasional pickup soccer game, and water bottles in glass, enamel, and stainless steel. Shit.

Before, things had been straightforward with Karr. Lewis saw him once, maybe twice, a year, and got his teeth worked on. Now Karr was friendly, wanted to ask questions.

"Ed," Lewis said. "What would you say to getting the nitrous started?"

"Sure." Karr looked where silver tanks usually stood. He frowned and called over Lewis's head to someone in the hall. "Molly?"

The blonde reappeared, said she'd be right back with the nitrous.

Karr turned and began opening one cabinet drawer after another. Instruments clinked. Lewis picked at a pin-size hole in his T-shirt. He stared at the corner where Karr's beige walls met.

"Mr. Dellmeyer?" He looked to see Molly staring at him. She was amber-eyed, with thick white blonde hair pulled into a long braid that ran down her chest. She inched a steel tank closer. "Ready?"

He nodded.

She gently positioned the gray mask over Lewis's nose, its two rubbery arms spreading in opposite directions. "How does that feel, Mr. Dellmeyer? Is that comfortable?"

He inhaled deeply. "Yes."

"Good." Karr clipped a white bib under Lewis's neck and buzzed the chair flat. Lewis drew in another breath.

Hands were moving above him, sharp instruments passing between Molly's delicate fingers and Karr's more muscular ones. "No, this," they were saying, and "Yes, that." All those instruments, Lewis knew, would end up in him. His mouth didn't seem big enough. His whole body, hardly big enough.

"Open please, Lew."

Karr smiled and Lewis sent a half-smile back, not to Karr's eyes, but his teeth, the whites of which looked uncomfortably familiar. Lewis felt his mouth open.

Another one of Karr's routines. First nitrous, then the needle. Lewis's head sank into the headrest, the base of his skull expanding. Karr stretched over him, holding the novo-caine-filled syringe just out of sight. "Quick pinch, Lew," he said. Karr's hand dove down and Lewis felt the slow jerked plunge in his gums. His forever-bleeding, forty-nine-year old gums.

"You all right, Lew?" Karr said, the needle still in Lewis's mouth.

His tongue had turned thick. Better to nod, Lewis thought, which he did. His head fell further back on the headrest.

"Ran into Helena and Toby the other day by Union Square. What's Toby in now, eighth grade?"

Here Lewis didn't nod. Didn't need to. He knew Karr would go on. And on. Last time, he'd talked about cycling. The problems with the Tour. Today, he started in about Toby. How he remembered seeing Lewis and Helena right before Toby was born, how huge Helena had been, not that huge was bad, and later, the surprise of running into the three of them at Mission Rock Cafe, Toby big and pink, Helena, exhausted. Understandably exhausted. He was all for kids, had plenty of kids as patients, but as for being a father, that he'd pass on. Marriage, too. Lewis didn't want to know why Karr had never married. Maybe he'd never found a woman perfect enough. Or liked to fool around. None of Lewis's business, really.

"But you and Helena," Karr said, "you've been together a long time. You have a good marriage."

He thought of Helena this morning, the tight line of her mouth wanting something. He'd forgotten to drive Toby to school. Big fucking deal.

"You're not the only one who's got to get to work, you know, Lewis," she'd said.

Suddenly he'd heard himself yelling, screaming things he

couldn't quite remember but knew for certain weren't too swift. Something about how she always had to have everything perfect, and if perfect was what she needed in a husband, she'd better go look someplace else.

The thing was he hadn't always been the kind of guy who screamed, but a guy who would, occasionally, leave a hot cup of Earl Grey on the nightstand so Helena could have it there first thing after she woke up, a guy who'd spent hours in Holly Park one Sunday morning riding Toby back and forth on his bike, holding the back of the seat until the kid could keep a wobbly upright going, a guy who once at San Francisco State—where he'd studied math for a hot minute before heading into construction—had stood outside Helena's dorm window in the night fog singing "Dear Prudence" at the top of his lungs just to hear her laugh.

Only this morning, he'd said nothing, nothing about the cracked tooth, his hours spent staring sleeplessly up at the dark ceiling. He'd just tossed the toast he'd burned in the trash and stuck his head deep in the refrigerator as if he were desperate for something. Toby yelled he'd get himself to school and slammed his way out of the house.

Tob. Tall for fourteen, tall and too skinny with a beaky face that, Lewis had to admit, looked a lot like his own at that age. He hadn't wanted Toby to storm out like that. But what could he do? Helena had launched in—why was he always shouting, always forgetting, so tired, irritable? She was sorry his father died the way he did, but why couldn't they talk about it? Just talk.

Lewis let the blue of Karr's eyes examine him. Talking was okay. Talking was fine. But yelling—he'd never say this to Helena—sometimes yelling felt so hellaciously good.

He sighed out a breath.

"Just another moment here, Lew."

He looked up to see Karr's face half-hidden by the hand he still had in Lewis's mouth. Pain shot up his cheekbone.

Last night, just as he was falling asleep, Helena had slid her palm along the small of his back, the faintly hairy triangle she claimed to love. All he'd been able to do was mumble, "Let's not," and move his exhausted body, his wrinkled dick to the far side of the bed.

"Should be fine now," Karr said, extracting the needle. "Good and numb."

Lewis blinked. The pain now was happening to some distant body far below his. *Numb* was not the word. *Good*, not the word. *Couldn't give a damn*, better. This was what he'd been waiting for.

"Ready?" Karr had put on thick magnifiers, glasses that blurred his eyes a darker blue.

Lewis motioned with his head yes.

"Close your eyes, Lew. You know, debris can go flying."

Colors floated across the back of his eyelids. Soft yellows, granular blue. Which turned into electric green. The drill had started up. The sound rose to a bone piercing whine that wrapped itself around his brain.

Breathe, Lewis, a voice somewhere inside him said. Not his voice really, but a weird combination of him, the nitrous, and what? He wasn't sure. Something bigger and at the same time smaller. But a voice he listened to when it got going in his head.

He inhaled.

Exhaled.

The colors faded and ran and shapes formed. Women. Long hair flying in the wind. Palm trees thrashing. Rain. *The National Geographic*, he remembered, the page open on the chair. Not the story about planets exploding, that other one. Women throwing themselves on a wet casket, faces twisted with grief. Men's arms holding them back. Men everywhere. Lewis felt his mind reaching backward.

"Turn a little to the right, please, Lew," Karr said. "That's fine."

Lewis turned, breathed. Now he was floating, sinking, bobbling again against the ceiling as if such a thing as a drill didn't exist, as if a dead father, an angry son, didn't exist. In. Out. In. His body hollowed, air filling his fingertips. He became a long tube of effervescent breath. His brain glowed.

"Suction, please."

When Molly used that dental thing to suck out his mouth, her arm touched his. Then, the soft tip of her braid. He couldn't help thinking about that hair, the light hair on her arms, the fine line he imagined running past her waist. Her pubes, were they blonde, too? Out of another darkness in his brain, something else rose, women, different women, lying on the thick, low branches of trees, all of them blonde everyplace a woman could be. He must have been all of fourteen, that magazine open, too, the page stretched so he could see everything. Lionesses, the women looked like, cheetahs half-hidden in leaves, ready to pounce, ready for anything.

Lewis felt something at the core of him swell, press against the zipper of his jeans. A nice firm press. Definitely firm. He would have smiled but a hand was in his mouth.

"A little wider please, Lewis. That's fine."

Then—his father had burst in, ripped the magazine out of his hands, thrown it across the room, his eyes glittering with anger. Or was it shame? His father's arms, Lewis remembered, the long dark force of them, the black hair.

This! his father yelled, spitting the sound, *This is how you spend your time! Well, time is something you're not going to have much of anymore, buddy. Time is going to get pretty scarce around here, what with all the chores you'll be doing, all the weeding and raking and mowing and hauling—*

Lewis felt hard bits of metal—or tooth?—hit the inside of his cheek. He closed his eyes tightly together. He wouldn't think about his father, the yelling, rage, disappointment. He'd focus instead on his tooth, what was left of his molar, caught in the light of the drill that was attached to an arm that was attached to a human being.

"Open your eyes now, Lew."

The drilling noise stopped, the air felt strangely empty. Lewis's eyes opened. He saw latexed fingers mounded in his mouth, Karr's brown head, and the edge of Molly's nearly white one. The light above his head glowed, the one-eyed light. He brought in another breath. His arms and legs softened, became as distant as the arms and legs of the two bodies moving around him. He remembered dead leaves and grass stretching across the lawn in perfect piles. Perfect, or else redone. Decades passed. Suddenly, it seemed, his mother called to say his father was in the hospital with pneumonia. Which by three o'clock the next morning had gotten worse. Much worse. Lewis blinked.

"A little to the left, please."

His eyes floated beyond Karr's. In the fluorescent diamonds of the light lay something. A question, maybe. A dream question, the kind you recognize instantly the moment you enter the dream, but always slips away as soon as you're awake. Lewis felt his lungs fill, rise like wings from his chest. He turned.

"That's fine." The drill started again.

Was this how his father had felt at the end? Turn left. Right. Open your mouth. Close. People leaning over him, pressing forward. No. Yes. Good. Fine. A white bibby thing under his chin, too. His father's mouth open, pink, no teeth, like a bird's. A bird too old and sick to bite anymore.

"Water?" Lewis had asked his father. He was surprised how much he cared. "Can I get you some water, Dad?"

No, nothing by mouth, the nurse had said. Not even water. Your father could choke and that would be dangerous, his lungs what they are. But when the nurse went off to wherever she was always going off to, Lewis couldn't help it. The old guy needed something. So dry and gray there in the hole of the hospital bed. His freckled hands on the sheet. *Here*, Lewis said, holding out some day-old 7-UP. *Only a sip, Dad. Just a little bit.*

But his father *had* choked, coughing, his face turning a violent purple, a color like blood but bloodier, his eyes bulging, his yellow hands jerking as if every little jerk was a syllable or a word or something that he, his son, should be able to understand, at least a little. Lewis was sure he'd killed his father, and all the nurses would come rushing in, see his father thrashing, swing their heads around and stare at the plastic straw still in Lewis's hand. *How could you do that? Kill your own father?*

Some blade-thin part of himself wondered if he'd wanted his father dead. That thought swirled through his brain. But his father had gone on to live two more days.

No—Lewis felt his brain light up—no way he killed his father. It was his father who'd tried to kill him! In the garage that time when he was a senior. About his taking off for Amy's, or the D in typing, or ramming the station wagon into the fence. One of those things, probably all of them.

He remembered the carving knife in his father's hand, still wet, shining under the fluorescent lights, the knife his mother had just washed up, so it must have been Thanksgiving or one of those sorry holidays when he was supposed to hang around all day and gratefully watch his father pour down one drink after the other until the littlest thing—a lost shoe, nicked door—would set him off, anger rising in his face like blood in a cut.

Only this Thanksgiving, Lewis decides he's taking off without a word. He turns to go but there's his father in front of him, yelling, *You get back in the house. Now!* Lewis keeps walking and suddenly his father's lunging, missing, missing, lunging, the sucker's so wasted he can't even keep the knife in his hand, metal clanging on the cold cement floor. His father's fist crashes into Lewis's chest, tumbling him to the floor so all he can do is *kickkickkick* at his father's skinny legs and Lewis sees how easy it is, how sad a forty-nine-year-old man really is, so he jabs his foot one more time good and hard and knocks his father over, their bodies rolling, heads butting, hands clawing, hitting mops, brooms, the lawnmower, all that rage down to the core spewing open and oh-so-fucking free, and before he knows it, Lewis is running, anywhere at first, then to Ocean Beach, empty this time of year, cold, where he spends the whole day and then night on the freezing sand, shells digging in his ears like broken teeth.

In the morning, he decides to go home—the old man has to be cooled off by now—so he picks up one sand-filled shoe and the other until in the distance he hears the whine of a motor. His father, for fuck's sake, is mowing the lawn, mowing like it's June and not November, making patient, straight rows as if his life depended on it, as if the grass isn't brown and stubbly, his father dead set against looking at him, determined to make this one day like any other.

"Lewis." Karr's voice sounded far away. "We're ready for the temporary. I'll just need a minute to prepare."

Karr's thick magnifiers were off, his eyes still and waiting. Molly had vanished.

Lewis adjusted the mask. "Okay, Ed."

But Karr didn't turn back to the sink as Lewis had expected. "I've been meaning to ask you, Lew." Karr buzzed the chair up some. "How are you doing?"

"Good." Lewis sucked in a breath. "We'll be done soon, right?"

Karr nodded. "I mean, since your father passed."

It took a moment for Lewis to register these words. *Passed*, he hated that expression. "Me? Fine."

"Are you grinding more at night?" Karr's tone was calm and insistent.

"I've always grinded at night," Lewis' shoulders rose. "Nothing new."

"Two cracked teeth in three months. Not a good sign, Lew."

Lewis looked at his feet, way down at end of the chair. He could almost see the dust from the lot where he'd been working yesterday rising off the tips of his boots. Karr had Weejuns at the bottoms of his legs, loafers polished to a high glow. Asking was one thing. But getting into his business, that Karr shouldn't do.

"I'm fine," Lewis said firmly. He watched Karr turn around and go back to work.

A question pressed up against the light, refusing to let him go. Lewis remembered staring into his father's mouth, the toothless mouth warped by the hard cone of the oxygen mask, the mask not yet removed. His father's green-blue eyes were flat, all the way open. And his chest: no rise, no fall, no nothing.

But was it nothing? Because his father's body was still there, his fingers up on the white sheet, the freckled hands Lewis remembered now not hitting, punching, grabbing, but magically reaching out to catch even the wildest pitch, the crazy balls he'd lob high over his father's head as a boy. His father fielded every curve, every furious grounder, all the pop-ups, and the up up and aways. Nothing had to be perfect then. The blue dream of night would come on, stars slipping between the trees, and still, they would play. Was that the dream last night? Lewis remembered hands, old, young, hands swinging forward, reaching back, one, then the other, and the other, and all the others until they became a fleshy blur, the satisfying dark *smack!* of the ball flying somewhere above so high and hard and sweet. He remembered his father's mouth laughing. Then open, there in the hospital bed. Refusing to close.

"Just another minute, Lew. You're going to like how this looks."

His boss had wanted him back on Monday, two days after the funeral. He'd had to practically beg for the rest of the week off, and when his boss finally agreed, he acted like he was so fucking swell. The house had to get up, didn't it? The windows installed, walls trimmed, joists rolled. "But you go ahead, Lew," his boss had said. "You take the whole week."

"Open wide." Karr smiled down, holding the tooth between his fingers

Lewis opened his mouth as much as he could. He felt Karr's hands again.

It'd gone fast that week. Too fast. People told him all kinds of things. Not just *Sorry*, but *He's at peace now. For the best. You're in our thoughts, Lew.* None of them had any idea who his father was. Who he—Lewis—was. Helena didn't know, her own parents were still alive and kicking. How could he explain—answer the questions she kept asking—when he didn't know himself? He kept trying to nail it, frame his feelings in hate.

Then the good would come.

The good would come when he was least expecting. The smallest thing could bring a memory on, the sight of a wild pitch across a grassy field, a collar flipped up against the wind, the wrinkles on the back of some stranger's hand.

Lewis blinked, harder this time.

When Karr fit the new tooth over the stump of the old, a sour taste ran down the back of Lewis's throat. He'd forgotten that bitter taste, tried not to breathe. But his chest rose and fell as if it belonged to someone else.

"You doing all right, Lewis? We're almost done here."

Lewis felt something wet roll out from the corner of his eye. It slid toward Karr's hand, his busy hand. Breathe, Lewis told himself.

Now tears were burning their way down his throat, dripping inside his ribs. Lewis twisted his fingers tightly together. This should not be happening. Maybe alone, or at home with Helena and Toby someplace downstairs. Not here. Not now.

A second tear slipped out.

Karr dabbed at the wet line with a corner of the white bib. He looked closely at Lewis. "Sure you're all right?"

Lewis stared up at Karr, his eyes wide and hard to read. Maybe old Karr wasn't so bad after all. The way he knew things. Lewis went to say something, but instead of a tongue he found a thick mass wadded in his mouth, dry as cotton.

"Yeah," he managed.

"Good. Let's let you clear." Karr switched the nitrous to oxygen, and lifted the mask away. The chair buzzed and suddenly Lewis sat upright, his ankles below knees, Karr's picture window stood before him again. The first tear fell in a crooked line down his neck, erasing itself silently under his gray T-shirt. The brilliant edges of Karr's wall turned into right-angles and beige surfaces. His once delicious breath became flat, ordinary. He couldn't feel half his face. But his fingers—Lewis tapped the armrest a couple times—his fingers were there. Spongy, but there.

"Okay, Lew. All set." Karr flipped the light up and away.

Lewis nodded, turning not toward Karr but the window. The branches growing against the glass looked different, darker green. It wasn't fruit hanging off them, he saw, but the buds of something just now coming on. A wind tossed one back and forth. Helena could tell him what these things were.

Helena. Lewis sighed. And Toby. They would be home before him, the house quiet. Too quiet. *Sorry*, he'd say, there in the living room or kitchen or wherever they happened to be. *I'm sorry about everything.* What they'd say back, Lewis had no idea.

He eased one foot out and felt for the floor.

Ask For Hateman

It's like there's this invisible wall between us. My father's still in the park, but now he's got this blue recycling bin in front of him. He pulls out a crushed Coors can, a Gatorade bottle, and a dirty wine jug, inspecting each carefully. He stares at me across the street—my heart nearly bursts through my chest—then away. Of course he doesn't recognize me. It's been forty years since we last saw one another. My father's grown thin, his face narrow and his beard white and scraggly. But his shoulders aren't hunched like you usually see in old men. He's wearing this floppy hat covered with buttons, blue, green, black all flashing in the morning sun. What looks like a leopard-skin thong sits twisted around the hat band. I want to walk across the street, but my feet won't go.

"Ma'am?"

The voice is deep and has a police-like authority. I've seen cops in the park, too, walking stiff-legged across the wet grass and hassling anyone who gets in their way. When I first turn around that's what I see—a policeman, this tall man in dark blue bearing down on me. Then I realize the deep-set eyes are staring more at one another than me, and his feet are half-shoved in their shoes and the heels bouncing. His legs stop moving for a moment and the eyes focus in.

"You have a beautiful chin," he says.

I've never thought of my chin as anything but bony, too skinny like the rest of me.

He nods. "You've been by. I noticed. More than once."

Back in Ohio, I was sure it'd be easy. *Just walk up and say, "Hey, Dad. It's me, Toni."* Or Smudge or Pesto or Briar or any of other names he gave me. Names I never heard out loud but read on postcards from California. I brought a few with Dad's ant-like black writing. The problem is I've been in Berkeley three days now and can't get any closer to my father than ten feet.

The tall man grins. "Why?" Now one of his big shoulders is jumping. "I mean, with ears like that."

What is he talking about? Chin? Ears? His sunburned fingers touch my arm but I don't pull away. He's strange, but strange I had been expecting. He's dirty yes, but his smell isn't bad, a musty too-long-without-a-shower smell. His hands are clean. He probably knows my father, the man the rest of the world calls Hate.

He left when I was seven, moved to California, and developed this philosophy, religion, ideology—nobody's quite sure what to call it. He used to stand on the steps of Sproul Plaza shouting *I hate you!* to people walking by. Amazingly, they laughed. After a while, a student reporter at the *Daily Cal* took notice.

"Hate is caring," my father told her, "as opposed to indifference. Indifference is the real problem."

Later, a journalist from the *Oakland Tribune* followed him

around for a day. "If we can be honest," the reporter quoted him saying, "straight about the negative feelings we all have for one another, then we can have a real conversation. We can care." A Hate Camp of six or seven—ex-Berkeley students, artists, homeless people—sprang up in the park.

"You tired?" the man says, still staring at me. "Because I am. We all are. What with life." He stops jiggling for a moment and smiles. "Maybe I could help."

I am so tired, but I shake my head.

"Where are you from? Nobody in Berkeley is from Berkeley."

This guy seems harmless, but still I hesitate. "Ohio."

"Where in Ohio?" he wants to know.

"Oh, this little town called Monroe." But the truth is I was born in New York City and lived there till I was seven. Monroe's my mother's hometown, the place where she moved us after my father left.. I don't feel like I'm from anywhere.

"I was from Milwaukee once. Now I'm from here. Berkeley's a lot better than people give it credit for." He stretches out a big hand. "Name's Krash. With a *K*."

I touch his palm. "You don't know someone called Hateman, do you?"

"Sure. Good man, Hate. Helps handle all the crazy shit that flows into the park."

"He's my—"

"Hate," he yells without letting me finish. "Hate! Someone here to see you!"

When my father turns to look at me, he doesn't seem surprised. He sits on a warped bench and motions to the empty place next to him, smiling at me blankly across the street.

My hair's short and gray now, not black and pulled into a long braid down my back. The last time he saw me, my face was pressed against our apartment window.

He waves at me again.

My heart starts banging in my chest, but now my feet take me across the street. When I enter the park, a man sits up in his sleeping bag, startled. Someone else keeps his head buried under a ripped quilt. I stick my hands in my pockets and keep waking. The air smells like incense and weed, heavy and too sweet.

When my father first arrived in California, one newspaper said, he rented a room off Telegraph Avenue. Then he camped out in the bushes behind Sproul Hall and slept in the corner of a friend's heated garage when it rained. But he was always in People's Park, arguing about hate and love. So thirteen years ago, he decided to move outdoors permanently.

"I'm not homeless," he told the reporter. "I mean if I didn't want a BMW, would you call me BMW-less?"

Alongside the bench sit my father's belongings. Safeway bags spill out of Whole Foods bags, a spiral notebook is flipped open to his black handwriting. Ashes fill two tuna fish cans to overflowing, and a pair of shoes lies nearby, one black, one white. For oppositionality, I know. Hate versus love. *Webster's Dictionary* with HATE CAMP Magic-Markered on the cover holds down the corner of a crinkled tarp. My father worked at *The New York Times* for ten years: first copy boy, then reporter, finally Metro Desk editor. Both newspapers made a big point of that.

I sit down on the bench next to my father. My hand's shaking so bad I have to hide it under my leg. Forty years. He pulls out a pair of green-handled scissors tied to his pocket with a string, snips off the filter of a Virginia Slim Extra-Long, and inhales. Deeply. He has that smoky *Dad* smell I suddenly remember loving.

He exhales a slow breath. "Before we begin... "

I know what he's going to say, I've read it. Every conversation has to start with *I hate you.*

"You don't necessarily have to mean it," he tells me, "but it'll be there when you need it. Which you will—sooner or later." My father goes on explaining, speaking quickly as if he's said just these words in just this way to thousands of people. And I'm just one of the thousands.

Until eight months ago, I didn't think much about my father. The ache of missing him had faded or maybe become part of me. But in June, my mother died. Cleaning out her house, I discovered a Keds box hidden under the bed filled with postcards my father had sent me. For years they'd kept coming, postcards from Berkeley that she'd never shown me. I found a file folder, too, of old newspaper clippings. I read everything quickly, feeling happy that he'd cared, then guilty as if my mother were right next to me.

Then angry. Why hadn't she told me?

I stared at the card of my father standing in front of Berkeley's Campanile, one hand perched on his hip and smiling. I thought, *Why not just take a week and see?* Without my mother living ten minutes away, life felt empty.

My father is still talking. Maybe I should hand him the postcard of palm trees and surf I'd brought with me. Or say, *Dad, stop. It's me, Toni.* But I still can't make myself reach through the silence of decades, the separation I'd assumed was permanent. Growing up, when people asked about my father, I shrugged. Sometimes I said he was dead. A missing father, that I didn't want to talk about.

But the man next to me looks very much alive, his eyes—the same blue as mine—bright. We have the same hair, too, frizzy at the first sign of rain. Finally my father stops, waiting for me. I tell him what he wants to hear, but it comes out muffled.

"Good, good." He smiles. "I hate you, too."

But sitting next to my father for the first time in decades, it's not hate I feel. It's not love either, just a strange kind of remembering. Not of this father, the one wearing a half-zipped sweatshirt and Mardi Gras beads, but the man in a herringbone coat staring up at the sky in Manhattan. The blue squeeze of sky between buildings. I remember the click and whoosh of bus doors, bright sun on ice, old men in elbowless jackets lying on top of metal grates, their newspaper blankets blowing, and my father takes me by the hand, steering me all the way around.

"So," he says now. "What is it you'd like to know?"

He thinks I'm a reporter. Of course. My red raincoat and new shoes, the black oxfords I'd bought for work. I calculate property taxes, talk with homeowners in the Warren County Assessor's Office. I've been there for decades. Not the most exciting job in the world, but steady.

A part of me wants him to think we've never met.

"You had a good life in New York, right?" I ask, trying not to sound nervous. "A successful career at *The Times*?" I pause. "A family."

He nods.

"What made you leave that all behind?" I've always wondered. What was the real reason.

"Drugs," he says, folding one knee close to his chest. "I'd have to say it was drugs." He tells me how this guy he worked nights with on the Metro Desk first got him stoned.

"I stayed high for like three days."

"Really?" I say, turning it into a question. I know this. I've read it.

He smiles. "Then I did acid. And whooooa. I realized there was more to life than getting ahead. Working night and day. At *The Times*, I was just grinding out what they told me to. The pressure not to fuck up was intense."

His mind melted, I overheard my mother say once.

"I thought if I could get that much pleasure from a single joint, or hit, or whatever, why was I busting my ass doing all these things I didn't want to do? Fuck it." Now he tells me what nobody in my family would talk about, but is all right there in print. The hallucinogens. Dope. He says he stopped getting high when he moved outside because he wanted to get there naturally.

"Now I'm addicted to fresh air," he says, lifting a white eyebrow. "Sun. What comes in and goes out of People's Park is incredible. But drugs are what got me started. I felt connected to everything."

"Everything?"

"Yes. Everything," my father says, giving me a funny look. "The experience was life-changing."

"What about your family?"

He opens his mouth but nothing comes out. His eyes look past mine. I turn to see a man in a gold helmet pedaling a bicycle, dragging two gold bins filled with newspaper up the street. He's strange, even for here.

"Hate!" he yells. "Fuck you!"

"Fuck you, too!" my father shouts cheerfully. The man gets off his bike and parks it against an oak tree. He hands my father a smooth white egg. The two silently touch palms, then the man bikes away.

My father lights another cigarette as if this is nothing unusual. One eyelid crossed with tiny red veins flickers the way it always used to when he smoked.

"Up until that point in my life," he says, ignoring my question, "I did everything I thought I was supposed to do. Got married. Cut my hair short. Worked my way up at *The Times*. I was making good money. But I'd turned into concrete. A real piece of shit. I had everything I thought I wanted: a nice apartment, a TV, a car. But I still wasn't satisfied."

I stay quiet.

"So I quit *The Times*. Left my wife," he says without emotion. "I started defying everything I'd ever been told. Even little things, like looking both ways when you cross the street. Except that was stupid. One day I got creamed chasing a Frisbee across Eighth Avenue in New York. I smashed my thigh and was in traction for, like, three months."

"You were?" This I had never heard.

He nods. "I woke up in the hospital the next morning and couldn't speak. Not a single word."

"What happened?"

"I had a complete emotional breakdown," he says intently. "Nothing in my life was working. My marriage was over. *The Times* refused to give me severance pay. Even words disappeared. I'd always had words."

My father sighs and his lips stay open for a moment. There's no teeth behind them anymore. His gums are empty, but I don't hear a lisp.

"In the hospital, you know, I had time to think. I'd always been in a big hurry, finishing college, finding a job, writing what other people told me to. For the first time in my life, I had a chance to really think." He lights another Virginia Slim off the one still burning. "That's when it came to me."

125

"What?" I ask, still hoping to hear about a daughter.

"I had to leave. Get away from everything. New York—the city I'd once loved—now seemed congested and completely contrived. As soon as I could talk again, I packed up and took off for San Francisco where life was freer. I never went back."

"You're kidding."

"Nope," he says with satisfaction. "Never."

Liar. Of course you went back, don't you remember? I remember. You, outside there in your battered VW, the engine idling, gasoline smells seeping through the corners of our living room window. For hours I watched you, your fingers tapping the steering wheel, turning the radio off and on. Bowie's voice wafted into the room, too. "Come away from that window," my mother kept saying. "You know I can't let you near him, Toni. I can't even let that man in the door, the way the he's gotten,"

My father blinks the smoke out of his eyes. I sit on one hand, and the other, watching myself become the girl who never questioned her mother so at least she"d stay. Someone who can't challenge the man next to her now.

He hugs his knee closer and leans back. "The park's amazing. I mean, by any sort of societal standard, I'm completely whacked. I say the *worst* things to people, *Fuck you. I hate you.* All they do is smile. *Have a lousy day!* I yell. They laugh. You probably think I'm nuts. But here in the park, I'm accepted. I've got my people. And I'm getting known in the world."

I can't listen to another word. I stand abruptly, staring down at my father's mismatched shoes. No one here—not Krash, not the man with the gold helmet, not any of the weirdoes he'd probably call *family*—even knows I exist. I'm forty-seven-year-old and they should know I exist. A police car speeds past, its siren screaming. A second one blasts by. I can't hear what my father's saying now, his lips are just moving, forming words I couldn't care less about.

"I've got to go," I say.

He squints up in the sun now overhead.

"I'm late," I lie. "For another appointment."

He smiles. "No problem. Come back if you'd like."

When I walk away, he calls after me. "Anytime. Just ask for Hateman."

What I want is to do is go home. Scan numbers at work, talk to people with clean faces. Take a long hot bath. I hurry down the crowded streets to Telegraph Avenue, walk through the door of my building, and take the agonizingly slow elevator up to the third floor. It's a dive, this place, full of rent-by-the week rooms that looked fine on the internet, a place I assumed had to be okay because it was just blocks from the university. But the walls are painted a too-bright white and the new orange carpet smells noxious. It's already buckling, rolling ahead of me in waves.

I unlock my door and pull the suitcase out from under the bed. Stop, I tell myself. Don't worry about it. Your father left a long time ago, remember. Decades. My shoulders ache. I call to reschedule my flight, ask for one leaving right away, but all they have is something in the morning. I pay the extra fees and book it. I fold a bright blue blouse in thirds—a blouse I thought my father would like but now will never see—and roll up a pair of gray slacks. Suddenly I'm exhausted. The bed's uncomfortable, but still I lie back. Then I'm gone, fast asleep it seems, because the eyes I didn't realize I'd closed, open. Noise is coming from outside. Metal on metal sounds, shouting. Could this be an earthquake? Wide awake now, I hurry to the only window, which faces the airshaft. Nothing looks wrong. The noise gets louder. I take down the stairs because who knows what might have happened to the elevator and push the big door open.

It's night now. The clouds have cleared, but no moon shines down. Dozens of people are walking up and down in the middle of Telegraph, banging on things and yelling. One man beats a white plastic bucket with a giant spoon, another clangs pots together, pots I remember seeing in the park. I look around for my father but he's nowhere to be seen. I stand on the sidewalk, feeling people push past me. A woman lights an overflowing garbage can and a long yellow flame shoots up.

Certain that plate glass will get smashed next, I spin around, heading back to my room. This is a riot, I think. People riot all the time in Berkeley I've heard.

But the sounds change, take on a kind of rhythm. A woman laughs. Looking back over my shoulder, I see an old man playing his shopping cart like a xylophone . Maybe this isn't a riot. It's a party—students in blue and gold T-shirts, homeless people, anyone and everyone taking over the streets. The fire flickers but doesn't flare.

A woman in a tinsel-threaded jacket smiles and hooks her arm in mine. "Don't just stand there," she says, pulling me ahead. "Join us!"

In Monroe, people only walk in the middle of the street during the Fourth of July parade and noise ordinances are strictly enforced. Tomorrow I'll be back there. But tonight—

The woman walks quickly and I have to hurry to keep up. The crowd folds in around us, teenagers with crew cuts, balding men with ponytails trailing down their backs, a woman pushing a stroller full of faded album covers. Boys play gray metal parking meters as if they were congas. The woman smiles and lets me go, pushing ahead.

I step in and out of circles of light thrown from the streetlamps above, people moving all around me. The shiny top of a head is illuminated, the back of a wrist. I pass shadowy shop windows, cracked doors. An old woman in pink curlers sits down in the middle of the street and drinks from something wrapped in brown paper. I move around her.

Out of a doorway, someone comes toward me with firm, slow steps. My heart lurching, I walk faster, but he matches my pace. I see a black shoe, a white shoe comes to meet it.

My father smiles, the corners of his eyes wrinkling. I know he's going to tell me to say *I hate you* so he can say it back. No, I decide. I'm not doing it. I'm not doing any of his hate stuff.

Without a word, my father reaches out and touches the gray in my hair. He looks at me. "Krash mentioned something about a woman from Monroe," he says, not calling me Toni, Smudge, or any of the other names he gave me. "Then I saw you just now. The way you tucked your chin in just like your mother—" His hand drops. "But older."

I pull away. Tonight my father's wearing a pillbox hat, an old Jackie Kennedy throwback, covered with big plastic daisies and pink blossoms, real ones. He's got on three sweatshirts, each collar dirtier than the next.

"Look," he says, his eyes narrowing with tension. "Your mother—" His voice trails off. "I *was* turning into concrete. Every day emptier than the one before. I had to leave. But that had nothing to do with you."

It's awful how long I wanted to hear those words.

He stops to and drags on his cigarette, then dives back in, saying how he was much too young when he married, how *The Times* brought out the worst in him, how he wanted to stay but couldn't, meant to send money but never had enough, a nonstop stream of justifying, defending, rationalizing.

He doesn't want me to hate him, I realize. The one person in the world who should, shouldn't. My stomach churns.

"I—I—" he's saying.

Those last two words sum up everything. A roar starts building in my ears and suddenly words are flying out of my mouth as if they were spring-loaded and waiting.

"You!" I yell. "Is there anyone else on the planet besides *you!* What about Mom, me? Or did you forget?" I'm zig-zagging now all over the sidewalk, pressing forward every time he steps back. "You think you're the only person in the world who's turned into concrete? Who feels empty?" I see myself in the dark shop windows beyond, my arms flinging wildly.

"Years!" I shout. My reflection dips in and out of the shadowy glass. Here, gone, like selves passing. "Where the hell were you?" I see the lonely seven-year-old, shy teenager, the woman marrying, divorcing, burying her mother. All the selves he never knew. Missed completely.

"I *hate* you, Dad! I mean it!" My legs are kicking, my elbows furiously jabbing air. But it's not pure hate I feel, but an unnerving mix of love, hate, fury, and sadness. So much sadness.

"Lark," my father says. "Wow. That was incredible." I can't tell if he's smiling with some kind of fatherly pride, or because he likes the new name he just gave me.

This man is your father, I think. Look at him.

"You wanted a real conversation, Dad," I say, my voice shaking. "Here it is."

"I hate you, too," he says, smiling.

His eyes move beyond my left shoulder. He touches one of the flowers on his hat as if to make sure it's still there. His feet start shuffling together and apart, awkwardly.

Five or six people have gathered, how long they've been standing there, I can't tell. Street sounds are still coming from everywhere, but right around us, silence. I see Krash's head above the group. The man in the gold helmet, now wearing pink high heels, stands on one side of him. On the other is a big woman with purple and orange dreadlocks. My father walks toward a man with his face is covered in tattoos. Chinese, they look like. The blue characters ride up and down his cheeks every time he smiles, which he's doing now, back and forth with my father. They exchange a soft *fuck you*.

Krash comes over to me, sucking on something that's definitely not a cigarette. He holds it out, but I shake my head. Everything's strange enough already.

He inhales deeply again. "You're back," he says in a tight voice, trying to hold the smoke in. "You and Hate connect?"

I nod. I don't volunteer that Hateman is my father and Krash doesn't ask.

He exhales a slow stream of smoke. "Don't know what we'd do in the park without him."

Try being his daughter, I almost say.

But Krash is gone.

A circle's formed around my father, everyone spilling into the center of the street. My father's got this plastic pail wedged under his arm and he's drumming it, drumming hard. His elbows are out straight and his knees bending so deeply it looks as if he might fly off. Krash pulls out splintered drumsticks from his backpack, and begins battering a chained bicycle wheel with no bicycle, completely off beat. The big woman twirls and twirls. I keep trying to catch my father's eye, but his face is always turned away.

GIRLS

1.

"Ma, it's 1965," Mela said. "Everybody wears one."

Her mother looked up from *Family Circle*. "Really? Every-one?"

Of course, everyone meant all the girls in sixth grade. Her mother didn't wear one, not that Mela could tell, anyway. Just these slips, white filmy things, with the straps always falling down.

"The school nurse says it's important we start out with the proper support."

Her mother didn't say anything.

She'd cried when Mela first got her period. "You're too young," she'd moaned when Mela finally told her. Mela guessed that meant she—her teary mother—felt too old. Twelve's not young, Mela thought. She'd been waiting to turn twelve forever.

But that night her mother had gone all out, made a dinner with all of Mela's favorites, tuna fish casserole with potato chip crust, peas but no carrots, pistachio ice cream. Even her father looked pleased, though her mother hadn't breathed a word, her wink told Mela that.

Still, she wasn't sure what the big deal was. She'd gotten her period, yes. But girls lied about that all the time. Lied they'd gotten it. Lied they hadn't. But breasts—that was the word the school nurse said they should use—those people paid attention to.

"I want to buy a bra."

"What about your undershirts?" her mother said.

Two weeks ago, they'd gone shopping for seventh grade. Her mother bought her a maroon A-line skirt, a good winter coat, and three cotton panties. When the saleswoman was ringing them up, Mela wanted to say, *a bra, too, Ma, a bra.* But she hadn't gotten up the nerve. Now school—the new junior high on the other side of Westport—was starting Monday.

"I'm too old for an undershirt."

Her mother smiled uncertainly. "All right, Pamela, if that'll make you happy, we'll go shopping. Soon."

But *soon* could mean weeks from now, even months. Definitely past the first day of school.

Mela walked into the kitchen, looking back only after her mother had turned into two feet stuck to a chintz chair. She looked down at her own feet. They were long and wide: boy's feet. Her shoulders, too broad. But her chest—*Carpenter's dream*, Tommy Gray had snickered in the lunch room. *Flat as a board*, another boy laughed.

She went out into the garage, climbed on her bike, and soared down the driveway and onto Shore Road. Beyond the seawall, the Long Island Sound glittered, light shivering across its blue surface. All summer she'd been swimming way out and slipping off her bathing suit. It felt good there, all alone, the water lapping softly against her shoulders, her feet stirring up the cool current below, the ocean silky all around. She could have stayed forever.

She pedaled hard in the direction of downtown Westport. As she got closer, she could see the town's single traffic light swaying in the breeze, blinking its summertime red.

"I've heard," Mela whispered into the rushing air, "I understand you specialize in—that your selection of—" The words had to be just right. As if she'd done this before. At the stop light, she imagined herself strolling into the store with confidence. She parked her bike and nervously pushed open the glass door.

She'd never been in the Village Shoppe before. Inside was one long white room with the cash register placed at the far end. All the clothing was covered in plastic. Dresses, pleated skirts, and button-down blouses hung on the racks in long shiny sweeps. Cable knit sweaters sat stacked in thick plastic bags, pairs of socks were displayed above in small sacks. Near the back, bras in translucent packages stood lined up in bins. Mela walked toward them.

The woman behind the register looked up. "May I help you?"

"I understand... My friend's mother said..." She forgot the rest.

The woman was old, past forty maybe. Auburn hair swept across her head and out in a stiff flip on one side. Wavy lines left by a row of bobby pins showed under the thick coat of hairspray.

"What is it you're looking for?"

"A brassiere," Mela said, trying to trill the r's like in French.

The saleswoman laughed, not a laugh, really, more like a sneeze or a snort. She wore an olive-colored shirtwaist dress with a thick tight belt buckled at the waist. She sat higher up on the stool and pointed her chest at Mela. Her breasts seemed like two beams of light focused on Mela. She couldn't help but stare. Her mother's were softer. But saggier.

"Don't tell me," the woman said, "that this is your first?"

Mela wrapped her arms over her chest. "No, of course not."

"No?" The saleslady walked Mela toward the back of the store. "Why don't you take the dressing room on the left?" She pushed aside the velvet curtain. "I'll be right back."

The fitting room was bigger than Mela had imagined, with two floor-length mirrors like in gym. If she angled herself just right in the locker room mirrors, she could see the other girls'. Some were even less than her barely developed chest. But Linda Thompson's were huge. It was scary how they almost stood up and spoke. *Bosoms.* That's what her mother had, too.

What did she have?

Mela slipped off her T-shirt. Two pale half circles of flesh looked back at her. Not *tits*, the word the boys liked. *Will you check out that pair?* Not *bosoms*, either. Not yet. *Breasts* wasn't right, in spite of the school nurse said. Maybe she should keep it simple. *Above* and *below*. Linda—someone she'd known since first grade—had a lush patch of dark hair *below*. Mela had, well, the bristly start of something.

"You do want a fitting, don't you?" a voice at the curtain said.

"Yes." A fitting sounded important.

The saleswoman entered, a frayed tape measure hanging around her neck. "Good. Now put your arms over your head. And keep still."

Mela tried not to breathe. The saleswoman's clammy

hands darted around her chest, brushing her skin here and there.

"Thirty-two and a third. Bigger than I would have guessed. How old are you?"

"Fourteen." People said all the time she looked fourteen.

The saleswoman sneezed out another laugh; this one smelled like burnt coffee. She carefully placed the cold tape measure on top of one nipple, then the other. Mela took in a quick sip of air.

"Only triple A in the cup." The woman smiled. "But don't you worry. That was me at your age and look how I blossomed out."

Mela's shoulders hunched. The saleslady's breasts pointed at her again, this time looking as if they might puncture the fabric. Mela couldn't help wondering what the woman had *below*. Was that red, too? Did pubic hair even come in red?

The woman's eyes caught hers in the mirror. "Mom busy today?"

"She's out." It was true. Today was her mother's bridge.

"I see."

"She plays tennis." Mela imagined her mother wearing a short white dress and boldly swinging a racket.

"Really." The saleswoman opened the curtain wider. "Lace or cotton?"

"Excuse me?"

"Lace or plain cotton? We carry both."

Mela dug inside the pocket of her cutoffs for the babysitting money she'd brought. Three crumpled dollar bills and a couple of dimes. "How much is lace?"

"Five dollars. Plus tax."

"Cotton, I guess."

The first bra slid easily out of its Maidenform box. Finally, Mela thought. Now Linda will be impressed. Her mother had taken her to get a bra in fifth grade.

"Lean over," the saleswoman instructed, "and shake yourself into it."

Shake? But Mela did as she was told. The first hook fastened easily. Standing upright, she managed the second. In spite of how hard she tried, she couldn't close the third.

"Takes some getting used to," the saleswoman said, catching the last hook for her.

"It's a little bit tight."

"Not a problem. Let's try another."

More boxes were brought. Bras began to accumulate, lying in a tangle on the cushion chair and hanging in bunches from the brass hook. Mela tried on a dozen or more. But the cups—stitched or smooth—always poked in, not out.

The saleswoman stood back and looked at her. "You know, the first one was best."

"Really?"

"It had lift. Support is important at your age."

"I know."

"Try it on again."

This time Mela struggled until the last hook met.

"A bra should be snug. It's good."

"It feels tight." She couldn't take in a full breath.

"Look, if you want a bigger selection, you'll have to go into New York."

The saleswoman sounded certain. Her mother never sounded certain. Her mother let her father boss her around. "It's *tartare*, Phyllis, not *tartar*," and "See you pick up my shirts from the cleaners" and "Please have dinner ready at six." Her mother always nodded. *Yes, Herb.*

Mela studied herself in the double mirrors. She loved

the way the white cups covered her chest, adding a layer. Maybe tight was how it was supposed to feel.

"I'll take it."

"Good. I will wrap it up."

Mela stretched the elastic band around her ribs. She undid and redid a hook. "No. Wait."

"Now what?" The saleswoman was walking toward the register.

"Could I wear it, please? Out?"

2.

Mela heard the sound of an engine and lifted her thumb higher. Cars had been trickling down from campus for over an hour now, drivers looking anywhere but in her direction.

"Please be a clunker," she whispered to the redwood trees overhead. Clunkers were a hitchhiker's best bet. But the wait hadn't been all bad, the Santa Cruz sun warm on her back, the ocean from up here stunning, a glittering blue triangle laced with fog. But the Pacific was anything but peaceful. Monstrous waves, violent rip tides. Nothing at all like the timid Long Island Sound. She didn't swim these days, she *plunged*. In and out of the numbing water as fast as possible.

The decrepit VW bus shuddered to a stop. A man with yellow-gray braids flashed her a grin and gestured to the back. The two golden retrievers dominating the front seat seemed to grin, too. Mela peered in the window. A guy with greasy hair driving a Thunderbird had picked her up last week. As he stopped to let her out, he'd slid a long finger along her breast. "Don't wear a bra, do you?" he'd drooled.

But this old hippie looked harmless.

"Thanks, man." Mela hiked up her long velvet skirt and

climbed in.

"Where you headed?" he yelled over the Beatles eight-track. *Everybody's got something to hide...*

"Downtown," Mela shouted.

"Cool." He jammed the bus in gear and it roared down the road.

Mela leaned back against the cracked seat. She rarely went downtown, but this trip couldn't be avoided. Her parents were flying in next week from Connecticut. Graduation. Commencement. Whatever. Her dress, cut from a faded Indian print bedspread, was all finished. She'd even embroidered the neckline with bits of shells to draw attention away from the weight she'd gained. It was perfect, except for one problem. You could see too much through the thin fabric. *Above and below.*

Her father would show up in his Westport usual: gray pinstripe, button-down shirt, black oxfords. Her mother would wear strappy sandals and a wraparound dress that revealed sagging breasts. Mela couldn't stand the thought of her parents staring at her, or worse, pointedly looking away.

She'd stopped wearing underwear of any kind freshman year. It wasn't just that women's underwear represented male domination. She'd never burned a bra, though she liked the idea of all that repression going up in smoke. No, the best part of *nothing* was the freedom, comfort. No more red marks ringing her ribs, shoulders, and hips. Mark liked it, too, the way he could kiss her all over.

She'd met Mark Lewis at the student co-op, a three-story gray Victorian on the edge of campus. He'd taken over the room not much bigger than a closet under the stairs, lining its single shelf with books like Marx's *Das Kapital* and Chairman Mao's *Little Red Book*. He'd even built a narrow bed that folded up neatly when not in use. She remembered him carefully easing down the wooden frame their first night together. That sweet, damp first night, his long body above hers, his hair a soft black curtain brushing the edge of her face. In the morning, he'd asked to look at her in the light, all of her. She'd laughed, slowly opened the crooked door, and walked through the house, naked. The two of them had sat nude at the kitchen table breakfasting on goat's milk and honey toast, his housemates giggling around them.

Mela looked down at the *V* where her thighs met. What would Mark say? She hadn't told him. She hadn't told anyone yet. She hadn't had her period since, when, April? Months, anyway. She crossed her legs and looked out the cracked window. Green slid by.

The VW bus slowed to a stop. "Here you go, sweet girl," the man said, turning around. "No smile for me today?" Mela clenched her teeth into a grin and pushed hard on the bent door.

Henderson's Department Store was one of those establishment establishments on Pacific Avenue where mothers brought kids school shopping, where tan and wrinkled women pondered cruise wear. A place so clean and evenly cool throughout it made Mela itch. Yellow smiley faces dotted the store windows.

Mela scratched and stared at her reflection in the sun-darkened glass. Wavy brown hair covered both breasts.

"If it grows, don't cut it," Mark said. He was right. Not just hair on her head, but also the blonde fuzz covering her legs and the dark growth under her arms. Well, no one in Henderson's could see. She'd made sure she was covered up: sleeves, long skirt, everything. She pulled the door wide open.

The lingerie section was filled with circular racks of white, pink, black, nude. The air smelled...*new*, was the only way she could describe it. A strange combination of starch, steam, and air freshener. What a trip.

"Could I help you?" The saleswoman's hair was dyed a dull gold, permed and cut short. She wore a black polyester dress splashed with pink flowers. Her smile reminded Mela of her mother's, uncertain of the creature standing in front of her.

"I'm looking for a bra that is—" She didn't know how to put it.

"Comfortable?"

"Yes." Mela exhaled. "Stretchy."

"Why don't you browse over there?" the woman said, pointing more confidently now to the center rack. "I just unpacked the whole lot."

Next to these soft fabrics, Mela's hands felt like bear paws. She knocked three plastic hangers to the floor. The quilted padding of one bra reminded her of a baby blanket. Others sported triple rows of hooks. She fingered a flesh-tone object resembling the top of a leotard. Extra large. It was worth a try.

On Mela's way to the fitting area, the saleswoman intercepted her. "I'll just unlock you a room."

The slatted door rattled when the woman closed it. The room was so small that Mela felt pushed up against the full-length mirror. In the dorm, she hardly glanced at herself before going about her day. Here she couldn't help but look. She eased off her blouse. She still hadn't found the right word for was reflected there. *Knockers, hooters, boobs, gazoombas, headlights, nay-nays, yazoos.* Sophomore year her boyfriend had named them *Little Suzi and her sister. Little* hadn't been appreciated.

Mela cupped her hands under her *breasts*, yes, that really was the best word. She examined them from different angles. They were...larger. Attention getting, and womanly. Thanks to the baby. But her thick waist and watery-looking thighs, those weren't so appealing. She looked more fat than pregnant.

Mela knew she'd been overeating. Finishing her senior thesis, "Gender-based Adolescent Initiation Ceremonies amongst the Shoshoni Indians in Northern Colorado," had been anything but easy. Eating took her mind off wondering if every bodily sensation might be a sign that her period was coming. Instead of nauseated, her appetite was voracious. She ate nacho cheese chips, Double Stuff Oreos, rocky road ice cream thick with chocolate sprinkles. Foods Mark would thoroughly disapprove of.

"Could I bring you anything else?" the saleswoman called.

Mela quickly slipped on a "Barely There." It was *there* all right. Who could wear these things? Mela's ribs were still too wide, even if her breasts were fine. Well, they had seemed fine a second ago. Grown up.

"Maybe something a little bigger...around the chest?"

"Of course," the woman said.

Mela listened to her retreating footsteps. She hated the idea of telling anybody. They would all start up: her mother crying, pleading with her to consider "all the options," her father yelling, and at some point, offering money. And Mark—

Mark would never let her alone. He'd make sure only the pure and organic passed through her lips. Raw chard. Rice milk. Rennetless cheese. She did love Mark, in a way. His long sweep of dark hair. The insistence and intelligence in

143

his eyes. But Mark could get a little bossy. He didn't like her shopping at Albertsons—"Mela, everything's covered in plastic. Even the apples." He didn't want her using teabags with strings. He even hated tennis—"Game of the ruling class." It was just *tennis*.

No, she had it all worked out. She could make it past graduation without anyone knowing. Then she'd hitch to The Farm. They loved babies at The Farm. Lots of mothers on their own there. She would phone Mark after she arrived. He could come to the birth, if he wanted. Stay afterward. Or not. Plenty of other men around. She'd already written the letter to say she was coming. All she had to do was mail it to Tennessee.

The saleswoman opened the dressing room door and handed her something. "We just got these in. It's the latest color. Mint green."

In spite of the hooks, Mela found it felt almost good, much needed support for her swollen breasts. The green reminded her of pistachio ice cream. If she had to wear underwear, why be serious?

"We're having a special," the woman said. "Three bras for the price of two. Matching panties half off."

"This one's fine."

"Why don't you give them a try? I'll be back in a minute." She turned and left.

Mela studied the price tag sewn into the bra. She knew the woman wanted to make a sale, but so? She was a working woman, a sister. Mela's parents had sent an extra check this month, an early graduation present.

"It's only money," Mark said. "A bourgeois obsession. Fucking money shouldn't rule the world."

Mela leaned against the glass sales counter as three pale

green bras and matching panties disappeared into crisp tissue paper.

"Good choices," the saleswoman said, pushing down on the keys of the brass cash register.

Mela smiled. "Thanks." She felt a sudden gush of fluid *below.* Something wet slid down the inside of her thigh. She handed the woman her check. "Would you happen to have a bathroom?"

The saleslady eased the tissue into a daisy-covered bag and shook her head. "Not one open to the public."

"I won't be long," Mela said, trying to sound as if it wasn't urgent. She felt another trickle.

"Oh, I suppose you could use the employee restroom. Just this once."

The woman led Mela past the fitting area to a small dark room. The toilet bowl was stained with rust. Peeling masking tape held together the cracked mirror. Mela sat down heavily on the toilet seat. Blood. Yes, blood. It seemed heavier than a period, but she couldn't really be sure.

A fist of tears tightened in her chest. She began to cry, cry without holding back. She leaned forward and sobbed in her hands. It had all been so perfect. Life after graduation. The baby. Now what would she do? Who would she love? She stared up at the stained ceiling.

"Is everything all right?"

Mela recognized the saleswoman's voice and froze. The toilet water was bright red. She had no idea how much time had passed.

"Yes."

"Well then," the voice said, "you can't stay in there forever."

3.

Before leaving, Mela checked in the mirror. No gray roots, at least not at the moment. She smoothed an eyebrow and tucked her colored-brown hair behind one ear, something she'd decided made her face look younger. She tucked in her blouse and walked toward the front door.

"Mom." Katie sat up the couch, staring at her.

"What?"

"They show."

"What shows?"

"Your boobs, Mom."

Not *boobs*, Mela almost said. *Breasts*. She bit her lip. She was the mother, after all. Someone who knew nothing. She sighed. Twelve was not an age but a disease. Where was the creature who used to trail after her saying "Uppie, uppie," so Mela would lift her daughter's small body? *I was your first food*, Mela wanted to say. *The reason you can feel a thing such as disapproval.* Well, Mark had something to do with it. Ever since Mela had moved out six months ago, Katie had been impossible.

"All right," Mela said. "If it'll make you happy, I'll cover up. Then leave."

Katie had been the one who'd urged Mela to schedule a professional fitting at Macy's in San Francisco: "Amy's mother did it. Now she looks so cool. Your underwear, Mom, needs to make it into the twenty-first century."

"Sure you don't want to come, too?" Mela asked.

Katie rolled her eyes.

Driving north on Highway 1 toward Stonestown Mall, the ocean appeared. Mela wound past oddly-shaped lagoons and wind-bent cypress trees. Beyond the cliffs, huge

waves swelled and spilled over. She imagined herself floating up out of the Volvo, flying high above the rough surf.
She wasn't sure who she was these days, or where she was
going. Being fifty-one was strange. Final in one way, but in
another, full of loose ends. Being fifty-one and single was
an even stranger combination. Like anchovy ice cream or
coffee served in a baby bottle. All Mela knew was that she
had to try living life without Mark. Without inspecting every food label for fat content, without rejecting any bit of
clothing less than one hundred percent cotton—or better
yet hemp—without raising heirloom tomatoes on the deck
every summer. Leaving Marxism behind after college hadn't
made Mark less rigid.

Whenever Mela tried to talk with Katie about what had
happened—how she wasn't angry, how she still loved Dad-
dy, she just needed time, space to see who she was, what
she wanted—her daughter shrugged. *Whatever.* One of her
favorite words.

After his first angry outburst, Mark hadn't wanted to talk
either, focusing their conversations instead on Katie. This
was not the man who used to argue about who should apologize for not apologizing first. The last time she'd dropped
Katie off, Mark had invited her in, offered a glass of the
homemade lemonade he and Katie had concocted with
Meyer lemons and wild mint from the backyard. The three
of them sat sipping the barely sweetened drink on his deck
as if everything were fine. Mela sighed. Maybe Mark had
started seeing someone. Discovered Viagra.

But so far, living alone wasn't bad. In her new apartment
near the Santa Cruz beach, the simple act of putting daisies
(Mark hated daisies) on the table instead of sunflowers (he
saved the seeds) gave Mela enormous pleasure. Last week

she'd played tennis with one of her interior design clients. Enjoyed it.

The mannequins at the entrance of Macy's Intimate Apparel department wore bras the colors of jewels: pearl, emerald, turquoise. Beautiful, but stiff. She'd never understood the appeal of underwire. Of course, it was all about support. Make the most of what you got: big, small, medium. She didn't fit neatly into any of those catagories.

The faceless figures wore panties in matching hues. Mela wondered what her less-than-firm hips would look like in one of these gems. A satin thong?

"Mrs. Lewis? I'm Joy. Your fitter today." The young woman wearing the plum-colored sweater and short black skirt smiled brightly at Mela's chest. Mela smiled, too, some. She'd taken the name Gray-Lewis when she and Mark finally married thirteen years ago, after living together, breaking up, then moving in again. She'd never been a Mrs. Lewis, but it wasn't worth arguing. Joy probably thought that The Beatles actually wrote that awful elevator music, that a hippie was something to be for Halloween. Joy's eyes looked around Mela, through Mela, as if her body were fading along the edges as she stood there. Joy was, well, *perky*, a word often used to describe young breasts. Two firm mounds rose from Joy's chest.

"Make yourself comfortable, Mrs. Lewis. I won't be a minute."

Mela sank into a chintz chair that reminded her vaguely of Westport. It wasn't just young women who treated Mela differently now. Men did, too. It used to be exciting getting in an elevator with a handsome guy, saying "Wow, that was fast," or when the elevator stalled, "Who knows where we might end up?" Watch him grin, or if she was standing behind, admire the back of his ears, the black hair lining the nape of his neck. She'd imagine them stuck between floors. Now men in elevators stared into their phones, clicked and unclicked the brass locks of their briefcases, impatient for the doors to part.

Her mother had once said, "You think it's hard being a woman? Try being an old woman."

Ma, Mela thought, *I wish you'd stuck around. I have few questions. Like, why didn't I appreciate my young body? Like, what should you do when you fall out of love? Stay? Go? You stayed. I left.*

Joy tapped Mela gently on the shoulder. "We'll be in the first room on the right. I'll give you a moment to get settled."

The fitting room was plush, not big but not small, its walls textured with iridescent diamonds. The hooks were white porcelain. Mela felt wealthy just standing there. One long mirror stretched her slim, a pleasing distortion. She kept her shirt on, knowing Joy would be back soon. Suddenly she felt nervous, sweaty in the crooks of her elbows and between her breasts. Her cheeks burned. Was this a hot flash? Maybe. Her periods had been wonky lately.

Joy knocked and opened the door without giving her a chance to respond. "Before we begin, Mrs. Lewis, tell me. What is it you're looking for in a bra?"

"Well, there's this one…" She must have purchased dozens of bras over the years: silk, rayon, spandex, cotton even. She'd tried strapless, racerbacks, demi-cups, sports numbers. All of them felt fine in the dressing room. But when she wore one at home, soon it was like a tourniquet tightening around her chest. Only this flesh-colored, worn-out thing, purchased years ago, and what she was wearing now felt good. The manufacturer had probably dropped the style long ago. "I'm not sure if they sell it anymore."

"Is it Maidenform? Jockey? Goddess?"

"I'm not sure." From the expression on Joy's face, Mela saw this was the wrong answer.

"How about size?"

"36B maybe?"

"Excellent. Let's measure you to be sure."

Turned out Mela was 38A. Another strange combination. Big where you should be small and small where you should be big. Most women wore 34B, she'd heard.

Joy returned, her arm dripping with rayon. "A bra should fit snugly," she said, handing Mela something nude-tone. "Adjust the straps correctly and the back won't ride up."

Mela nodded.

"Support is important at your age."

"I know."

"No..." Joy hesitated. "Let's go with this one first." She held out a gold-colored bra. "Lean forward and let your girls fall into it." Girls? Mela thought. But she slipped off her shirt and did as Joy said. When she straightened up again, two contoured foam cups stood up stiffly on their own as if they held nothing inside. Joy stared at Mela's chest and imperceptibly shook her head. "I'll be right back."

Mela fumbled trying to get the slippery fabric on the plastic hanger, then finally gave up. She turned toward the mirror—her new apartment didn't have a full length one—and looked.

Her breasts had shrunk. Being pregnant with Katie, of course, had changed everything. Silvery stretch marks shone under the fluorescent lights. She'd enjoyed being buxom, but it didn't last. Her nipples were now long and flat, like permanent pink stains. Mela pushed up both breasts with her hands. The skin felt silky and cool.

"Mrs. Lewis?" Joy called.

Mela slipped on a bra, any bra, and opened the door.

"We just got this in," the young woman said, holding out a silk undershirt. No, not an undershirt—*a French camisole*—Joy corrected, in a rainbow of colors. All of them had hidden bras. "Aren't they terrific?"

Mela had to admit they weren't bad. Colorful. Enough coverage to avoid embarrassment. Supportive, too, if you didn't mind feeling smothered in organic silk. She looked almost attractive in the mirror, breasts swelling above the V neckline. A much younger version of her much older self.

How was that possible? The pace of change was relentless, her body advancing toward some unknown but absolute endpoint. It'd been easy getting pregnant after she and Mark married, too easy. This had not done wonders for their sex life. She had never told Mark, never told anyone, about that time at Henderson's Department Store, the sudden gush of fluid, the blood and tears. Maybe she hadn't even been pregnant. She'd never know for sure.

"Now *that* looks great." Joy stood at the dressing room door holding a stack of camisoles. Pistachio, champagne, and cinnamon-colored, she said. "Delicious, don't you think? And a wide variety of colors to choose from."

Impulsively, Mela decided to buy three. They were nothing like the ribby white undershirts, she told herself, the ones her mother made her wear as a girl. Tight, but didn't they have to be?

"That's how you know they're *doing* something," Joy had said.

The young woman tapped the purchase into the thin computer. Mela watched as she encased the garments in silver paper and slipped them in the starred bag. *These are camisoles*, she would tell Katie. *French camisoles.* Her daughter would probably still call them old-ladyish.

On her way out, Mela passed racks of gleaming underwear, counters with circles of coral and pink lipstick. She walked quickly, unsure if this was the way she'd come in. She started down a new aisle. This one displayed boots with thin high heels and purses hanging from silver chains. Up ahead, a row of glass doors appeared, the light glowing green across them.

The light would be like that when Mela pushed through the doors again, this time moving in the opposite direction to return the camisoles. At home they'd turned out to feel increasingly uncomfortable. Tight and somehow cloying.

Joy didn't recognize her. "Could I help you with anything else?" she asked from behind the cash register.

Mela shook her head. There seemed no point in reintroducing herself.

As she turned to go, the aluminum sales counter shimmered, burnished circles spinning away and away. Out of somewhere a memory rose, water lapping against her twelve-year old shoulders, her feet touching the cool currents below, her arms threading back and forth. How hard she had to work to stay afloat, how for a moment the ocean seemed all hers.

RESTRAINT

My father's hand is out of the restraint and the oxygen
mask dangling around his neck. The plastic cup tilts out,
spilling air. He's bunched the hospital gown above his waist.
For the first time in my thirty-four-year-old life, I have a
clear view of something I'd only glimpsed before. Out of
the uncircumcised folds runs a catheter, the inside coated
a dark yellow.

His hand swipes at the tubing.

"Dad, stop." I quickly cover him with the sheet and
tighten the mask over his nose and lips.

My father grumbles and turns toward me, but his wrinkled eyelids stay closed. His chest and shoulders heave with
the enormous effort of breathing. The plastic fogs for a
moment, then his breathing calms. I pull the Velcro tabs
apart, but cannot bring myself to bind my father's wrists.
The restraints are soft white pads lined with terrycloth, but
still—restraints.

I go look for help.

≈

Yesterday, I found my father sitting up on his own, the

green strings of his oxygen mask tucked neatly over his ears. Someone had shaved him and combed his thick white hair, but parted it on the wrong side.

"Dad," I said, walking into his room. "How are you?"

I didn't think he'd answer. My father had been on a ventilator for a week, and the doctors had just removed it the night before. The CCU physician had told us his situation was hopeless, though his cardiologist had never said that. Instead he talked to us about ejection fractions and flabby heart tissue. My mother and I prepared ourselves for the worst. But after my father was off the ventilator, rather than dying, he got better. The nurse monitoring his vitals that night was amazed.

"His Pulse-Ox is within normal limits," she'd told us at two that morning. "Best we've seen."

My father's lips began moving around what looked like words. I leaned closer. His eyes seemed lighter blue, almost crystalline at their centers, and his skin glowed as if it were backlit. I stretched the oxygen mask away.

"You know," he told me, sounding surprised himself. "I feel pretty good." His voice was hoarse but perfectly intelligible over the oxygen's hiss.

I pulled the hospital chair close. "You do?"

He nodded. "Ready for a few more rounds."

I laughed for first time since I left my husband and eight-year-old daughter a week ago in Bakersfield. I'm the Assistant City Manager, a job people say I'm good at, a job I like. Here, I dutifully drive my mother and myself sixteen blocks to the hospital and back, talk with nurses, and occasionally a doctor. It's so mindless that it seems my other life doesn't exist. March in San Francisco is freezing.

Dad and I watched a football game on the muted TV

the way we used to when I was growing up. But instead of screaming at the screen, now he was quiet. His forehead wrinkled as he tried to follow the players' push down the grid. When I looked again, his eyes had closed. His eyelashes were pale—almost invisible—I hadn't looked so closely in years. His hand felt cool to the touch. I rubbed the calloused palm and his skin warmed.

He started talking under the mask. I bent toward him.

"I said, I'd like to know who your father is." His eyes looked sincere.

"My father? Why?"

"I want to compliment him on his daughter."

It took me a moment to understand and when I did, my throat tightened. Part of me felt happy. Another part, angry. It wasn't me he'd complimented, but someone he'd just met.

❧

The nurse comes in and places the restraints around my father's wrists. "We don't like to use these things," she says, "but last night he kept trying to get out of bed. Has he ever been—" She stops and studies me for a moment. "Would you be able to sit with him tonight?"

She doesn't say the word *combative* but that's what I expected. Because he has been "combative," as she'd put it. And not just here.

My mother got the worst of it. My father never left a mark that I could see, but still scared her so bad that she flinched whenever he came up fast and close. I remember a bloody nose once but don't remember how it happened. My mind backs away.

Mom wants to visit Dad in the hospital just once a day. She darts forward, kisses him quickly on the forehead, and

155

retreats to the corner like a small white bird. She opens a book, then falls off to sleep.

Me, he was easier on. The fact is he never hit me, maybe because I was a girl. The only girl. But he'd scream, his face so close to mine I could map the broken capillaries on his cheeks. "Can't you do anything right!" he'd yell. Anything could set him off: missed homework, poorly parking the car, dishes stacked wrong in the dishwasher.

When the house was quiet again, he'd find me in my room. We'd all go out to big, fancy restaurants, The Blue Fox or Alioto's. There I'd get to order anything, two of something even. Plus dessert. I remember the table crowded with half-eaten cuts of steak, crumbling blackberry pie, soupy ice cream.

I became the good girl, the never-good-enough girl.

"Sure," I tell the nurse. "I can come back tonight."

෨

The CCU is dark when I arrive. It took longer than I'd expected to settle my mother down for the night, get her tea with lemon, and click on the rerun of ER. Walking down the hall of the hospital, I pass a mix of real and television sounds coming from half-lit rooms: a voice saying *Hello? Hello?*, a machine thrumming, the scream of police sirens.

My father's body looks bigger than this morning, his face younger as if all the oxygen has pushed the wrinkles out. His foot with one sharp toenail hangs off the bed.

The faded Polaroid I'd brought in sits next to the tray of untouched food: apple juice, beef broth, and Jell-O with a dab of hardened Cool Whip. I break off a sliver. In the photo, my father hovers over the Christmas pot roast, seeming to relish the knife he's holding and the holly-covered apron he has on. His mouth is open, telling a long-forgotten joke.

"Hey Dad," I say, trying to sound upbeat. "How are ya?"

My father's eyes flickers, but his hand keeps inching to the right. Now he has hold of the restraint and is trying to work it off. I push his arm away. "Don't do that, Dad, okay?"

His mouth wrinkles into a frown. I recall the nurse saying if I'm right here the restraints aren't necessary. I loosen the warm bindings. After a while, he dozes off and I open up my novel.

His leg twitches under the hospital blanket. My father turns toward me, his lips open as if he's about to talk, then he turns away.

"Want something?" I nudge the mask higher on his nose. The light behind the bed shadows his eyes, and my hand over his face darkens them more.

Sounds of movement come again. When I look up, I see my father has kicked off the thin blanket and is struggling to swing his leg over the bed. His eyes are disappearing circles in his face.

"I'm late," he says.

"Dad. You're in a hospital. This is a hospital."

He swings the other leg over. I put my fingers on top of his. "Go to sleep." He bats at me with his free arm and misses.

"You'll hurt yourself, Dad. Come on. The tubing." I gently press on his chest so he'll lie back.

"Get away!" The hand flies up again and hits me in the face. My cheek burns. I think, *He wants to do this, he likes to do this.*

"Get back to bed!" I shout in a voice that's all too familiar. It's not just the voice of my father that I heard growing up, but the one I find myself using with my daughter when she won't do what I say. A voice that sickens me.

Still I scream. "Now!"

My father falls back on the bed, breathing hard.

The nurse rushes in the room, stopping at the foot of his bed. She looks from me to my father, his eyes big and wet and weepy above the mask. "Is everything all right in here?" she asks. Her voice has a forced calm.

I nod quickly.

She picks up the loose restraint on the bed, opens it, and slips my father's wrist in. "Maybe it'd be easier if we used these tonight?"

I blink as if I have no idea what she's talking about.

Just Go

Lyn stood outside Lipstick, the fem bar on Harrison, staring at the lot of dead Muni buses next door. Some looked whole except for a crushed window or torn off door, other were just used-up carcasses of aluminum. She pulled out a Camel from the pack she'd just bought, struck three matches before lighting the damn thing, and drew the smoke deep. She finished that cigarette and lit another. Sofia would disapprove, but Sofia would be late. She was always late coming off a shift in the ER. Lyn smoked the second cigarette slowly, ground the butt out on the sidewalk, and headed into the bar.

Inside, Lipstick had its familiar glow, the rows of liquor bottles backlit in blue, the hanging glasses coated pale yellow. The jukebox was softly spinning out "Crazy."

Lyn leaned back on the barstool, letting her eyes adjust. The oval mahogany tables were pushed together in twos and threes, and gold confetti littered the floor. Last night must have been one long celebration, but right now the place was empty. Just her and this old gal in clean work boots sitting way down the bar. Nothing more depressing than clean work boots, Lyn thought, especially this time of day. It was just two in the afternoon. She would have been gladly at work—pulling wire and installing electrical sockets—if not for that noon appointment at the medical center.

"Tanqueray," she said to the bartender. "Rocks." As soon as the gin arrived, she drank it.

"Another?" the bartender asked.

"In a sec." She wanted to feel this one hit first, reach into her bones, fill her breath.

Because she didn't want to think about something else settling in her bones. She hated the thought of the doctor bringing her back in. "Just a few follow-up tests," he'd say. "To be sure." Even a few were be too many. No, she wanted to get out there on the shadowy dance floor, drag the old gal out, too, get the bartender to put on Etta, Aretha, the Gaga woman even, make the music so loud it buzzed their ears. She wanted to dance herself silly, kick and groove and spin.

When the bartender wagged the bottle, Lyn nodded, then danced her way toward the WOMEN'S.

The old gal, who was watching the Giants game on TV, grinned at Lyn as she got closer.

"How's Zito doing?" Lyn asked, stopping alongside her. She was wearing an orange and black ball cap, her gray hair swept up in it.

"They need to get him out of there."

"You sure?" Lyn stared up at the screen. "It's only the second inning. He could work his way out of it."

The old gal shook her head.

"Anything's possible," Lyn said, dancing her shoulders a little in the mirror behind the bar. "This is baseball."

The woman's smile got bigger. But when Lyn came out of the ladies room, she was gone.

An hour later, Sofia arrived. "I'm so sorry," she said, kissing Lyn briefly on the cheek and sounding somehow cheerful. The ER at UC San Francisco was usually crazy, but today, Sofia said, the place was insane: defibrillators going blooey, an old man taking a swing at a security guard, other physicians' pagers going unanswered and unanswered. At the end of her shift, a two-year-old came in from a car accident. "The little girl had a compound fracture and Mom was already headed to surgery. I just couldn't leave her."

"I know." Lyn downed the quarter inch of gin left in glass, tilting away from Sophia. Her lover had a nose that could pick up day-old smoke on a sweater, much less two fresh cigarettes. Fuck, Lyn thought. For two years, she'd been so good. Followed every one of the doctor's rules: low fat everything, no more than half a drink twice a week, forget even a single cigarette.

Sofia stared at Lyn but said nothing, settling down on the barstool alongside her. Though they were both thirty-nine, Sofia was the one who looked older, her blue eyes lined with dark wells from working long hours, the curly black hair she almost always kept pulled back patched with gray. Lyn's brown hair was straight and thick, fully grown back after the chemo. She'd gained back the weight she'd lost, too, her waistline spilling now over the top of her Levi's.

"Hey," Sofia said. "How did your visit go?"

"Fine," Lyn lied. A routine six-month, that's all it was supposed to be. She knew something was wrong when the technician suddenly got quiet when just the moment before she'd been all breezy.

"Good to see you again, Mrs. Skyler," she'd began—why did they insist on calling her Mrs.?—she'd never married anyone, including Sofia.

The woman kept chattering as the exam started. "Sorry, I know. Cold. Big breath here. Hold it. Beautiful. Keep holding. Good. Good." Lyn breathed and didn't breathe as instructed, watching the gray boom lower over her left breast, her only breast. Out of the blue the tech said, "Excuse me," and quickly exited. She came back in the room and took another set of films. In silence.

"Is something wrong?" Lyn finally asked her.

"The doctor will speak with you."

"Can't you tell me?"

"I'm sorry," the tech had said, with a weak smile.

Now Sofia asked her. "Did they say anything?"

"Blah blah blah. Have a nice day."

"I'll check for you. The results should be up by now."

"No." Lyn reached for the glass and remembered it was empty. She wished she felt drunker. "They'll be in touch."

They met at a 2010 Giants game, three years ago. Lincecum was on his way up then—Boy Wonder, Freak—and the bunch of them sitting behind first base started high-fiving any hand put up there in the excitement of what might be another shutout. Lyn's seat happened to be next to Sofia's and they got to talking about bobblehead giveaways. There'd been Sandoval, of course, looking way too svelte, and Bochy and Mays coming up. Those ridiculous heads and skinny arms, weren't they great? Weird, but great. After the game, Lyn and Sofia kept talking, talked all the way up the stairs and through the gate until they were standing next to Lyn's orange Camaro in the parking lot, still grinning. Lyn was attracted by Sofia's muscular calves and delicate wrists, and Sofia—she said later—by Lyn's square shoulders, and her easy, sometimes sarcastic, laugh. The red cowboy boots hadn't hurt. That they came from different worlds—Sofia a physician, and Lyn an electrician—didn't matter. They both loved baseball, the sheer grace of the game that burst wide open when the pitching went wild. Which it usually did by the sixth or seventh. And they both loved to dance. They danced in bars and clubs all over San Francisco: Badlands, Wild Side, The End Up, partying late the night the Giants clinched the 2010 World Series.

That next spring, they bought season tickets together, meeting up for dinner together at Delancy's before the game, or heading off to Momo's afterward, where Sofia nursed one drink and Lyn plowed through three. They discovered Lipstick and hung out there after work.

When Lyn's cancer hit, their time together suddenly was filled not with baseball and drinks, but doctor visits, MRIs, and chemo appointments, all of which Sofia managed. Glad to, she said. After the surgery, Lyn opened her eyes to see Sofia floating above her. "It's over," Sofia told her, smiling. "Your margins are clean." The next time Lyn woke up, Sofia stood alongside her bed adjusting the IV. Celebratory ginger ale arrived. The next day a steak appeared, overcooked but still Lyn's favorite cut. After her discharge, Sofia drove Lyn straight to her townhouse to recover.

When Lyn was up and around again, still at Sofia's but feeling better, she started cooking up a little dinner for them to eat together. Nothing fancy: spaghetti, chicken stir-fry, cube steak, but God, it felt good to be cooking again. Next she fixed the flickering light in the living room. Afterward, Sofia kept switching the thing on and off. "You make that look easy. I just assumed I'd just be stumbling around in the dark forever."

Sofia stopped and looked at Lyn and Lyn looked back.

Neither of them said anything but both of them knew. Lyn returned just once to her studio apartment in the Richmond, and that was to pack up. The place seemed too small, too much a part of the illness that, as the months passed, almost felt as if it had never happened at all.

❧

Two weeks after the latest mammogram, Lyn stood in the kitchen, the room in Sofia's house she'd most made her own. She had installed two sets of track lighting on the ceiling and hung a stained-glass lamp over the breakfast table. Sofia would just as soon eat Grape-Nuts out of the box or ramen in the dark—habits she'd picked up as an intern. But in this kitchen with its long granite counters and stainless steel everything, Lyn loved to cook. Especially when her mind felt jittery.

She peeled a white onion and forcefully cut it in eighths, then sixteenths, and scattered the pieces in the frying pan. She smeared butter over a roasting chicken with her fingers and pulled out a package of wood-smoked bacon from the refrigerator. Tonight, she was going to eat, and not one bit low-fat. Sofia had arrived home an hour ago from working back-to-back shifts, and was in the shower.

They'd argued. On the phone and again as soon as Sofia had walked through the door. About the results. About what to do next. Everything. Though neither said anything, both knew the shower was just an excuse to get away from each other. Lyn gathered the broken onion skins in her hands and dropped them in the compost pail under the sink. She laid a bunch of carrots on the cutting board and started to peel one with quick, rough strokes.

The next time Lyn looked up, Sofia stood in the kitchen doorway, her hair wrapped in a thick white towel.

"Smells great," she said softly, unwrapping the towel and spreading it across the top of a chair. "When's dinner?"

She ran her fingers through her water-dark hair, the curls falling around her hands. Instead of iodine-stained scrubs, Sofia wore a blue T-shirt and plaid pajama bottoms now, tied at the waist with a tight bow.

"Won't be ready for a good hour yet," Lyn said more harshly than she'd intended. Not only had they pinpointed a tumor on the left, a spot under her collarbone had been discovered. The oncologist at UCSF, a gray-skinned man she'd never met, sat her in his office and talked about invasive globular this and estrogen positive that, saying the treatment wouldn't be as easy this time. Lyn felt herself nod, as if to say, Sure, it'd been easy before, exhaustion so bad she couldn't get out of bed—much less work—skin where eyelashes and eyebrows used to be, just skin, and a scar crawling like barbed wire across her chest, sure, all that had been a walk in the park. When he finished, she'd stood up, and walked out of the room with a strange sense of calm. Which was gone now.

"Lyn—"

"I told you, Sofia. I don't want to."

Sofia opened her mouth, then closed it. "But—" she said, pausing again. "Why not bring Webber in? Get his opinion? He knows your history, tolerance levels, everything."

Webber had been Lyn's oncologist two years ago, a physician Sofia knew from Stanford. The three of them crowded into the small exam room together as Webber—everyone called him by his last name—said, "Let's hit this thing hard. Knock it clear out of the park." Lyn's nod then had been genuine. Not once during the tortuous twelve months of treatment—chemo followed by surgery followed by radiation—had Webber used the C-word. Lymphocytes, locoregional, lesion, yes. Lead off, strike zone, screw ball, lots. He loved baseball maybe even more than they did. But he and Sofia also threw around all kinds of impossible medical jargon that Lyn didn't even try to decipher. She'd felt like shit. They were doctors, weren't they? she'd thought. Let them take charge.

Not this time. "I don't want to involve Webber," Lyn said with determination. "Not now."

"Okay," Sofa said. "All right. Webber's not an expert in Stage 3, anyway. That's what we need right now. There's this new guy in Onc. I'll shoot him an email."

"No."

Sofia came and stood close to Lyn. "What are you saying?"

She wanted to—just go. The two words had floated to the top of Lyn's brain as she was driving down Parnassus after the visit this morning. She didn't know what they meant, not really, not yet. A part of her was still catching up. She just knew she wasn't going back again to the gray–faced man at UCSF, or even the baseball-loving Webber.

"You know," Sofia said. "Stanford just started a new clinical trial—"

"You're not listening to me." Lyn felt she couldn't breathe. Not because of the cancer. The doctor said she'd probably feel fine for a while yet. Her markers sucked, her scan was a mess, but she felt fine. She just couldn't breathe at the moment. Lyn inhaled forcefully. "No doctors."

"You can't mean that."

"I can," Lyn said. "I do."

In the silence that followed, Sofia walked to the other side of the kitchen and opened a cabinet filled not with cereal or pasta but bobbleheads. All the bobbleheads they'd collected together. There was Cain, Romo, a couple of Lou Seals, and Eckersley. Eck wasn't a Giant, of course. But still, an amazing pitcher. Sofia had given Eck to Lyn after her first NED—No Evidence of Disease—result.

"Lyn," Sofia said. "Listen. A forty-five percent survival five years out isn't bad. In fact, all things considered, it's good. Really good. Almost fifty-fifty."

Lyn stared at her. "What the hell are you talking about? The doctor didn't give me any percentages." All the oncologist said this morning was *Given recent advances, it's likely you'll still be with us in two years.* Still with us. Shit.

"It's in your chart."

"You've been through my chart?"

"Yes, I—" Sofia's voice dropped. "Wanted to check."

"I don't believe it." Lyn made herself breathe. The last thing she wanted was Sofia taking over again.

"You didn't mind before."

"I gave you permission before."

"And you're not now?"

"No. No!"

"Please don't shout," Sofia said with deliberate calm. "Lyn, honey. What you have is absolutely treatable. Every note in the chart says that."

"Stop!" Now she *was* shouting. "Don't you see? What I have may be treatable. But it's not curable. The doctor made that perfectly clear. Tell me, Sofia, how long did I get between treatments? A year maybe? And after this? Six months? Four? What is the point? I don't see the point."

Damn if she'd let them poison every cell in her body, watch her body turn the color of dead grass again. Walk around feeling as if she had the world's worst hangover without the pleasure of a night's drinking before. Not this time.

"Sweetie. You just got the news. You're in shock. It will go away."

"Do not fucking tell me it will go away." When Lyn fixed Sofia with a hard stare, she felt something shift inside her. Distinctly move from here to there. Whatever she'd been circling all day—some decision, plan—became clear.

"I'm going to do nothing."

There, she'd said it.

Lyn walked to the stove and turned over a strip of bacon in the pan using her fingers. She couldn't remember the last time she ate bacon. On chemo, food turned to sawdust. Food brought nausea. Lyn turned over another strip, not feeling it burn at first. She rushed to the sink and ran the cold water until her hand felt numb. The skin turned bright red.

"I don't understand," Sofia said.

"What's to understand?" Lyn shook the water off. "I'm going to let things take their course. Nobody lives forever. Nobody." She felt certain about something else, too. This time she sure as hell wouldn't be good.

"Why don't we talk in the morning," Sofia said. "After we've both had more sleep."

"No, I take that back," Lyn said, as if she hadn't heard. "I am going to do something. Eat." She passed Sofia the cutting board with carrots waiting to be cut.

Later than night, Lyn dozed on and off in front of the TV as Lincecum battled it out with Sabathia at Yankee Stadium, both pitchers subpar this season. The next time Lyn's eyes opened, the screen was filled with a gold cat dancing on tall thin legs, then big glossy lips, then a wrinkled man cheerfully holding up a green pill, until suddenly—she wasn't sure how—there stood Lincecum in the middle of the screen, a still, pale expression on his face. Runner after runner crossed home plate. That's it, Lyn thought. The season's over. Sofia would be optimistic, she knew, open to any possibility. But as far as Lyn was concerned, the Giants were finished.

She stumbled down the hall to the bedroom where Sofia lay asleep, still curled around an open book, her body a soft, breathing shape in the dark.

Lyn lay on the far side of the bed. At midnight she was still awake, staring into the shadows hanging over her head. She rolled from her back to her side, turned on her stomach. She coughed and worried they had missed a spot on her lungs—she pictured it as a splotch of pink dirt. She saw her body changing from its fleshy self to bones barely able to draw air. In spite of how easy it'd been this afternoon to think about—going—now her mind veered away.

"Sofia." Lyn touched her fingers.

Once that was all it took, a touch, and they were kissing, deep calm kisses that soon took over. Sofia's skin felt impossibly good against hers—slick and warm and surprisingly strong—bringing her pleasure after pleasure. But since Lyn's diagnosis, they rarely reached for each other. Even then Sofia avoided Lyn's chest.

Other times, too, not when they were making this cautious kind of love, but when Lyn was getting dressed for work, or naked a moment before bed, she felt Sofia look at her, staring at what was now just scar over rib. Instead of taking Lyn in as she once had—eyes filled with desire—now Sofia turned away, with guilt or shame, maybe; it was hard to tell. Then she covered her own two small breasts.

"Sofia," Lynn repeated softly.

"Be right there," Sofia said in a doctor-like voice and rolled over, already back asleep.

Lyn lay in the dark a while longer. Finally she stood up and put on her Levi's and a cowboy shirt trimmed with turquoise. The streetlight hung in the window like a half-moon.

❧

Lipstick was so crowded, she had to fight her way in. The parking on Harrison Street had been nonexistent and the lot next door filled as usual with broken down Muni buses. When Lyn finally made it through the door, the bartender was all the way down the bar pouring out three margaritas at once. "Whole Lotta Love" blasted out of the jukebox.

Lyn pushed impatiently through the crowd, smelling lavender and sweat. A calf brushed against hers, then someone's shoulder. All these women, she thought, the twenty-something tatted wonders, the seventy-year-olds with spiky silver hair, not one of them knew. Not one of them would look at her with serious eyes and ask how she was feeling. Or worse, say how fantastic she looked with voices full of forced cheer, smiling anywhere but at her chest. She was passing, not for straight now, but for healthy.

Lyn reached the bar and waved, trying to get the bartender's attention. A hand touched her arm.

"Hey didn't I see you in here the other day?"

At first, she didn't recognize the woman wearing green flannel shirt and a silver nose ring, grinning at her. Then—of course, the old gal. Except tonight she didn't look so old. Her hair wasn't tucked up in a ball cap, but spilling over her shoulders in blonde and silver. And her work boots looked great, dirty from a long day's work. Lyn remembered the affair she'd had before she moved in with Sofia, a brief fling

170

with a contractor she met on the job, a woman Sofia either hadn't noticed or deliberately didn't mention.

"A week or so ago?" the not-so-old gal said. "The Giants were on?"

Lyn smiled. "That's right."

"Boy, do they suck. I mean, after winning the whole damn thing last year, what the hell are they doing now?"

Lyn nodded emphatically.

"My name's B.A.," the woman said, as if they were just picking up the conversation. "How've you been?"

"Fine," said Lyn, looking away. "Good." When she looked back, the bartender was standing in front of them with one eyebrow raised like, *All right, ladies. I don't have all night.*

"Can you make me a chocolate martini?" Lyn asked.

"You bet." The bartender turned to the woman.

"Same."

Lyn leaned her elbows back on the bar and B.A. stood facing her, legs wide apart. They talked about nothing, just the way Lyn wanted to. How it was the extra splash of vodka that made a chocolate delicious, how work was picking up for women in the trades. A little. They ordered another round. And another. When Lipstick's band, the Clicks, started to play, the music got so loud they moved closer to be heard. Tonight the dance floor wasn't shadowy, but crowded with women, their hair—frizzy, blue, blonde, dark—lit in the spinning lights. Lyn watched an arm shoot up, somebody jump.

B.A. whispered in her ear, "Dance?"

Lyn followed her to the dance floor. The beat picked up and B.A. moved closer. Lyn felt the pulse of her shoulders. And hips. B.A. did this slidey thing with her knees. Lyn did it, too, adding arms overhead. They traded moves back and forth. Just danced. She hadn"t felt this good—this drunk—in forever. Lyn kicked off her boots. The wood floor had just the right slip on bare feet.

She and B.A.—Did they really? Yes, they did—danced the hustle, funky chicken, a deep Elvis twist, all toes and hips. Her mother had taught her that. The mother whose grave she always got lost trying to find in Oakland's Mountain View Cemetery. Lyn closed her eyes and pushed that thought—all thought—out of her brain. She swayed her hips, bent her knees, pumped her elbows, feeling the music work its way deep inside. Sweat filled her back. When the band stopped and the lights came up, Lyn felt stunned for a moment by the brightness. Then she looked around, but B.A. was nowhere to be seen. Lyn headed out the door, still barefoot.

"Hey you." B.A. stood in a group of smokers around a pine tree twinkling with lights. "That was fun," she said, holding out her drink.

"Really fun," Lyn said, taking it. She lit her own cigarette off B.A's.

Through the blur of smoke and clouds—blurrier still for the vodka now warming her chest—stars appeared. The clouds separated for a moment and between their silver edges, more glittered.

"Wow," Lyn said. "You never see stars like this in San Francisco."

"Nice, isn't it?" someone said.

"Yeah," B.A. smiled. "September can get like this. Clear. Look, even some of the Milky Way tonight." A faint band of white twisted across the sky.

"May, occasionally, too," the voice came again. Then Lyn

knew. Sofia. Instead of looking at her, Lyn dragged hard on the cigarette. When she finally did meet her lover's eyes, Sofia's brow tightened.

Lyn shrugged. The last thing she wanted tonight was to feel guilty.

The woman stuck out her hand cheerfully. "Hi there. I'm B.A."

Sofia frowned. For a second, Lyn thought Sofia might do something. Yell, carry on. Maybe Lyn wanted her to. Stop being so goddamned nice.

"Hello." Sofia smiled.

"B.A.'s for Betty Ann. But nobody calls me that. " She gestured to Lyn. "And this is—"

"Lyn," Sofia said. "I know."

"You two know each other?"

"You could say that," Sofia said.

At first the silence that followed seemed simply a lull in the conversation, but as Lyn kept her eyes focused any-where than on Sofia, and as Sofia's frown deepened, her hands fidgeting with the keys in her pocket, the buttons on her shirt, anything, the tension grew until the night air felt thick with it. Lyn ran her finger around the rim of the martini glass and licked off chocolate.

Inside, the band started up, an especially soulful version of "Valerie" vibrating the air.

"Let's dance out here," B.A said. "It's too hot inside." She began to move her hips, slowly, then faster. She reached up and waved her arms. To Lyn's surprise, Sofia joined her.

Though Sofia loved to dance, she wasn't all that good at it. Tonight she looked especially klutzy. Doing a horrible freestyle funk, she began flailing one hand as if her finger-nails had caught fire, then bobbling her head. B.A. grinned.

This only seemed to encourage Sofia more, who smiled, too, turning her foot on the sidewalk as if she were grinding out a stubborn cigarette. B.A. danced closer.

Lyn watched with resentment, her eyes moving from woman to woman. B.A. caught Lyn staring and stopped.

"Is everything all right?" The song was winding down.

Lyn exhaled a long stream of smoke. "Fine."

Sofia stopped dancing, too.

"Oh," B.A said, as if the word held a special significance. She turned toward the bar door. "Why don't I just—"

Before Lyn could stop her, B.A. left.

The two of them stood on the sidewalk in silence.

"I want you to know," Sofia said finally. "You are a complete shit."

Lyn flicked the extinguished cigarette at the blue disabled sign, but missed. "I just wanted to dance, that's all. Have a couple drinks, without you there judging me."

Sofia continued. "At first I was sure you were in bed next to me, fast asleep. Then I thought, the bathroom. Or the couch. I even searched the coats in the front closet. Why, I have no idea. I opened the front door and stood out on the porch. An orange car drove by. Then it dawned on me. Of course. Here."

"I couldn't sleep."

The shadows under Sofia's eyes looked darker than usual. "Me neither."

Lyn felt the liquor burn under her ribs. She stared down at her feet. They looked bigger and uglier than she remembered. A bump on her toe stood out grotesquely.

"It's been a long day," Sofia said. "Let's go home."

"No," Lyn said.

Sofia's fingers brushed hers and Lyn pulled away, lurching at first in no direction at all, then heading toward the cemetery of old buses. She started to run, spurred on by the alcohol.

She swerved through the narrow fence opening, then between the buses, their windows splintered and dark, the doors jammed open, or missing completely. Metal sides were bashed in. Her heart crashing in ears, Lyn remembered a different set of walls, the hard plastic so close she couldn't move. How many MRIs had she had, her arms frozen over her head, her body buried inside the machine? She ran down another row of buses, turned, headed in the opposite direction. Sofia was somewhere close behind, she could hear but not see her. Lyn jumped over a crushed beer bottle, severed wires. She realized she blamed Sofia—the conscientious physician—blamed her more than any other doctor, for all those tests, the agony of chemo, and its failure. Blamed Sofia, too, for loss of years that Lyn, in spite of this afternoon, felt now owed her. Thirty-nine was young, wasn't it? Much too young to just go.

"Lyn," Sofia called. "Wait!"

Lyn flew between the gray buses, her breath coming in sharp bursts. Another memory surfaced, this one of long after the surgery, long after radiation, too, her burn marks nearly faded. She and Sofia sitting on opposite sides of the couch, full from the dinner Lyn had just cooked, the sweet flan dessert. Suddenly she'd wanted to talk about—what? The nothingness, her fear of nothingness, the erasure of everything she knew and was. Who would remember her after sixty years? Who? They'd be dead, too. She hadn't been able to find the words that night, words useless anyway in the dark face of it.

Lyn continued running, the buckled pavement sharp

against her bare feet. She slipped in another row of metal buses, running, slowing down only to speed up again. Sofia was darting somewhere behind. The night floated around her, stars rising and falling, the moon blurring in and out of view. She smelled the oil-stained concrete, the bay's salty air. She stopped, but her body kept swaying.

The sounds of Sofia could no longer be heard.

Because she was right here, stepping out of the darkness, so close Lyn could hear her breathing. Sweat-soaked curls haloed Sofia's head. Her hair had been like that the first night they'd spent together. Loose, impossible, beautiful.

Lyn turned away. "The last thing you need is a complete shit twenty-four-seven."

Sofia pulled Lyn close so that every part of their bodies pressed together, hips, ribs, breasts, heart, so they could feel their lungs lifting for breath.

"No," Sofia said. "The last thing I need is no one there at all."

For a long moment, Lyn wanted to let go. Then, she didn't.

VOICES

Don't you remember that afternoon, April maybe, the afternoon that at first didn't seem so different, you and I in the art room painting on the big black sheet a huge yellow eye streaming spikes, an eclipsing sun, a bird rising, a full moon? We mixed spit and eyelashes in the paint; I insisted that a fortune-telling booth needed a few human ingredients. I felt a little silly, nervous really. We had out your mother's big book on palm reading, but who were we to tell the future? You, you had something else on your mind, something I sensed when I looked up, saw you staring at the sky beyond the school windows, the Chappaqua sky shredding clouds.

"It's late," you said. "My mother should be here by now."

"I'll drive you home, Mike." That's what we used to call each other, remember, Mike and Ronnie, not Catherine and Anne? Boys' names to fool the boys who liked to snatch the tightly wadded notes we passed in the hallways and stairwells of Horace Greeley High. Names we allowed ourselves to say out loud only when we were alone as we were then—two long-limbed, yellow-haired seventeen-year-old girls born on the same day of October. Why those particular names? I don't remember. I just remember how good they felt in my mouth, how their straightforward sound made us seem more alike. Because we were different, too, in ways we didn't talk about. Your family had money: a grandfather was the head of Standard Oil or something, your father worked in his firm in Manhattan. Your mother called you her "one and only." You summered in Hyannis, got a clothing allowance. I was the third of five. My father took us camping in Maine, my mother assigned chores.

We closed the book, hung up the black sheet, and climbed in my rusty VW. You looked out the car window, quiet as usual, and I stared ahead, quiet for once. The silence of Chappaqua's back roads stilled me, the pale beginnings of spring drawing me in until your white house appeared on its grassy hill, a revolutionary eagle screaming over your front door, like all the front doors in your sought-after part of town. I dropped you off as usual in front of the garage and slowly backed down the tricky curve of your driveway, my head turned, so at first I didn't see you.

See you jumping, your feet hanging loose from their ankles, jumping these strange little half jumps, helpless jumps I'd never seen before and never saw again. Smoke oozed under the garage door as if it wanted at you, too. Your arms were frantic motions of up-up-up, and your mouth, what I remember most is your mouth, a noiseless circle in the full moon of your face, a circle that became wider and took on sound as I rammed the car back up your driveway.

"Mommmmm," you were yelling, "Mmmaaaaa-mmmm."

Decades later, your voice still rings in my head, that word, which must have been your first, sliced in two, the word that now sliced our lives in two, the sound of *Mom* soaking into the us that was then and the us that was to be. You again, last night, another dream. Here in this house in San Francisco, not New York, in my bedroom where the moon hangs over the oak trees. My husband softly snoring beside me, my twelve-year-old daughter sleeping down the hall, and suddenly you appear. You've been stealing into my dreams for months now. I want to know what's calling you back.

The dreams are not of this, not of what happened to your mother that afternoon in 1968, but everyday dreams, nothing special. A face. A body crossing the room. Your body crossing a room, a room in a house I've never seen. A white house, two stories. You're wearing a brown hat, a silk scarf floats behind. I follow you, surprised, happy. *Mike, Mike, it's me, Ronnie. I didn't know you were here.* Your back's to me, you keep walking. I follow you from room to room. Maybe you can't hear. The music? "God Bless the Child..." Maybe I should call you Catherine? *Catherine. Cath.* Finally on the stairs you turn to face me, eyes huge. *Go away. This has nothing to do with you.* Then I can't find you. Grimy dishes piled up block my view, books stacked on the countertop. I can't find anything.

Only we did find her, your mother, that afternoon. Together we managed to open the garage door and rushed in, coughing. The yellow-gray clouds of exhaust were heavy with gasoline. I saw the blurry outline of your mother in the front seat of your red station wagon, her hands resting easily on the wheel. When she slowly turned, her eyes seemed to swirl with smoke, emptied of blue. Finally, she cranked down the window, crank by excruciating crank, and peered out as if we were the one who were ghosts.

"Unlock the door, Mom," you screamed. "Get out!"

"Catherine? You're all right?" Your mother's words came

out as if she were speaking underwater, bubbles rising from her lips.

Not seconds, but centuries went by before I reached in and lifted up the lock, so easy now, and you slipped your mother from the still running car, through the gray drifts, and out into the April sun. I stayed with her at the top of the driveway. You went back in the house to call an ambulance.

In my first memory of you, you were standing just outside the swirl of bodies at a middle school dance. "Wild Thing," a song we'd heard too many times, echoed off the gym walls. The boys stood in bunches, hands hidden in their khakis. In the far corner, girls danced in two and threes. The music was so loud people yelled, or said nothing at all. You were wearing a lemon-yellow dress and sandals, one long leg casually bent, as if you were about to step forward, or back.

You were tall—too tall—like me. When the music changed to a slow dance, the boys didn't approach us. Their heads reached only our shoulders, or worse, our chests. From opposite sides of the gym, I watched you watching everyone else. Your face was smooth, your blonde bangs precisely cut. The perfectly plucked arch of the eyebrow made me look away. My stick-straight hair was chopped short, my skirt a dull plaid from last year's sale rack. I was known for talking too much and about the wrong things: astronomy, how much things cost, trees. We'd seen each other before in the halls, of course, but still I was surprised when a few weeks later you called. "Want to go shopping or something?"

Later you'd tell me you liked the way I talked. The way I could go on without worrying about what I was saying, or how I was saying it.

180

At the top of your driveway, words poured out of me. What was taking so long for the ambulance?

"Are you all right, Mrs. Parks?"

"Can you hear me Mrs. Parks?"

Your mother, as if she could barely feel her body below her, just stood there.

"Do you need anything, Mrs. Parks? Water? Crackers? I can get you something, you know." My voice took on the urgency of a plea, a whine.

The ambulance drove up, the doors opened, and two men got out, men who called her Constance... One held out the oxygen mask and she accepted, slowly bringing the green cone to her face as if it were an exotic flower, delicious. She took your hand and gracefully climbed into the back of the white and red van.

"Mom," you said, patting the seat, "here." I remember seeing you and your mother framed in the rear window, your shoulders close but not touching. The ambulance pulled away, no lights, no siren.

I argued with myself all the way to the hospital in Mount Kisco. *Cath's mom just started the car and forgot. Happens.*

It was your father, back suddenly from the city, who had to make it clear. In the Emergency Room, dark now, the three of us waiting for the psychiatrist to arrive.

"A psychiatrist?" I asked. "Why not a regular doctor, Mr. Parks? Don't you want her to get checked?"

Your father looked at me, his face as smooth as yours, but his voice annoyed.

"Yes, a psychiatrist." Glancing at the white door behind which your mother waited, too, he added, "Look, Anney, we appreciate everything you've done. But maybe it's time you leave. Just family now."

When I got home, I told my mother what had happened.

"Really? I'm sorry," she said, continuing to sponge out the sink. "Mrs. Parks doesn't seem the nervous breakdown type. Happy enough. All that money." She wiped her hands with a dishtowel. "Have you eaten dinner?"

"No," I said.

"You should eat."

"I'm not hungry."

"I saved you a plate. Eat."

❧

I've never told you, but after the ambulance took you and your mother away, I went back into your house. I closed the car door and entered the big room off the garage. It seemed like your mother was just upstairs, about to come down. Dishes sat stacked in the sink, half-folded laundry covered the back of the sofa, a book lay splayed face down on the floor. The brown boxy radio next to the television was turned on. Loud. Hissing static, stuck it seemed between stations. Voices broke through the crackle, words clear, then lost again.

I'd never thought about your mother before. She'd just been a voice rising and falling on the phone, a pot clanging on the stove, a silent plate of almond cookies, a mother who, unlike mine, didn't mind the music up loud. But in that empty room she turned, became for a moment someone who listened to static, who needed static to become voices, voices to become commands, commands to be what she must do: shut the garage door, start the engine, lay her hands on the vibrating wheel, and wait. Wait for the voices—those, yours, maybe even mine, wait for everything she touches, and is, and might be, to be still. I pushed the thought out of my mind.

❧

On my desk at work I keep a small stone, a rock you painted. A blue sun wraps its face around the indented surface; the eyes are warped, the yellowish lips stretched big. Orange paint has chipped off one eyelid. I found it in a box with old charcoals, water-stained books. I like to run my hand over its surface, trying to remember when you gave it to me. I can't. You were the one who began painting, not me, the one who painted everything: canvases, cups, stones, silk. All I have is this. Occasionally a colleague will stop and ask, "What's that?" I pull my eyes away from the computer and see how old the thing looks, how dated. Sometimes I say, "A friend made it for me. A long time ago." Sometimes I even out notebooks at the back of my desk, shrug. "I found it somewhere, liked the way it looked." How can I explain?

❧

We only talked once about your mother being in the hospital that first time. The two of us were in the front seat of the same red station wagon, driving back from White Plains, Bloomingdale's or Lord & Taylor. On the road home, you turned to me, your eyes paler green in the afternoon sun.

"Up there. That's where my mother is."

I followed the trail of your long finger and saw a brown mansion on a hill, a black fence wrapped with blooming roses, red spilling over the sharp posts.

"Oh," was all I said. The way that big house silently capped the hill, no sign anywhere, and the way you looked away, your words opening and closing the subject of your mother in the hospital, I knew that was all I should say.

When your mother came home, she seemed all right.

Better, really. I saw a new fullness to her waist, a silver chain added to her glasses. At first, I walked carefully, kept my eyes down, worried that just seeing me might bring that afternoon back for her. But your mother's eyes, fresh and fully blue, sought out yours, mine. She cooked us coq au vin, Welsh rarebit, dishes I'd never tasted before. We sat on flowered chairs in your dining room, the maple table so polished I saw my own face looking at itself. At my house, we ate at the kitchen counter on vinyl stools. Someone always had somewhere to go: a basketball game, choir practice, Cub Scouts. My mother made us sloppy joes, fish sticks, tomato soup from a can. Foods that kept.

On her fiftieth birthday early that summer, your mother baked a pistachio cake and topped it with strawberries.

"No candles," she said. "Might set the house on fire." We laughed and ate the whole thing—one third, one third, one third.

"Never thought I'd ever get this old," she said. "But here I am." Fifty seemed impossible to me, too. Your mother made herself a pot of percolated coffee and drank only one cup. The rest would go to waste because your father was working. When I started asking questions—not about that, but "Why do some people put salt in cellars, like your family, Mrs. Parks, and others in shakers?" and "What's the difference between teal blue and teal green?" and "What makes bone china bone?"—your mother listened intently. She rose from time to time to consult the big dictionary on a wooden stand in your living room, turning the tissue-thin pages until she found answers I don't remember. What I do remember is that after dinner she wanted us to look at the moon.

"Girls. Come see," she called.

She held the door open, her body half-in and half-out

of your screen porch, pointing as if she were responsible for that pale creature caught in the dark tangle of summer leaves.

"Can you see the man in the moon?" she said. For the first time I made out a blurry face with brown eyes like mine, the mouth open either laughing or crying, I wasn't sure. Laughing, I decided.

"In China, they see a rabbit. In India, a horned bull. Depends," your mother said.

"On what, Mrs. Parks?" All I knew of the nighttime sky came from library books.

"Yeah, on what, Mom?"

"On who's looking. On what we want to see. A face, an animal." She paused. "We're what the moon wants us to be, too."

"Mom."

"It's true, Catherine." Your mother stepped towards us and I felt my shoulders shake a little. I found this kind of talk exciting.

"The moon has more influence than people realize," she said. "Take menstruation. Have you noticed that your periods change according to the phase of the moon? Start? Stop? Get heavier? Lighter? You girls are old enough to talk about this now." Your mother raised one arm and let it fall. "Whatever made the moon made us."

I'd never seen my mother do more than glance up over her head, too busy taking care of us, she'd say. She found my interest in astronomy strange for a girl. My mother couldn't bring herself to say the words *menstruation* or *period*. It was *those days*, or *your time*, as if something more precise might make her mouth itself bleed.

You looked worried. I stared up at the black sheet of a

sky, the white hole the moon had punctured in it.

"It's cold, Mom," you said. "Let's go in. *Laugh-In*'s on."

"No, it's not," I said. "It's not Friday."

"Anne," you said nervously, "remember, the special?"

"What is the moon made of, Mrs. Parks?"

"Anne. Come on."

"That's right," I said. "Goldie Hawn's special."

Your mother laughed. "Well, then. *Laugh-In* it is."

You went in last, carefully closing the screen door so it didn't bang.

Streets clog with bits of white time. Moments disappear. The *us* then seems not to have anything to do with *us* now. I look at my arm on my desk and think the flesh could never have been smooth, the skin clear. Lines have worked their way into the backs of my hands like faint hieroglyphics. When we were seventeen we leaned into the wind of time, pressing everything forward. On. Now I want it all to hold still. Go back. We'll be forty-nine next month, you know, not even close to the age your mother had been.

Our last year of high school, 1969, we were not Mike and Ronnie anymore. We became Cath and Anne. The world was changing, and you and I with it. The hair we had had so precisely cut now grew out in profusion. Hair hid our eighteen-year-old shoulders, reached our back ribs. But eyebrows, legs, underarms, those we continued to meticulously and painfully pluck and shave, tweezers on the sink, razors edging the bathtub. We wore mauve coats with fur collars, skirts so short we couldn't bend over, skirts so long you couldn't see our feet. We twisted feathers in our hair. We didn't talk about your mother much. She seemed normal,

acted normal, she faded. We were the ones, the birds rising, the full-faced moon. The future wasn't a black-sheeted
booth, but a sky sprung wide open.

The nickel bags of weed, do you remember? Five dollars for an inch of crumpled green. Your hand passed a
clumsily wrapped joint to mine, which passed it to another,
which passed it to another and another, till it came back to
you again. Circles so solemn they seemed almost sacred.
Your eyes glistened under the man's hat you liked to wear,
a brown hat tied with orange silk scarf. You leaned back in
the sweet, sharp smoke, giggling. Me, I couldn't find my
voice. I felt myself falling, nothing to catch hold.

Stoned, we walked in the woods behind your house.
Peeling white birches. Giant sycamores casting big hand-
shaped shadows on the dirt. Boulders, saplings growing in
cracks. *Ashes, ashes,* you sang.

"Let's close our eyes. Be blind," you said when we
reached an open field. "We won't fall down." I cheated,
watched you edging forward, arms out, touching nothing.
Later, we found a long, low rock and sat. I picked up a
flat stone, gray with quartz veins, and flung it between two
trees. It bounced off the thick grass.

"If this were an ocean, we could skip these," I said.

You picked up a brown rock and threw it. It wobbled
and landed next to mine. "Yeah, but then we couldn't see
where they ended up."

The rocks piled themselves close to one tree. In the
shadows, they looked like an open mouth. Not laughing
this time, I thought. Crying.

"Did they ever figure out what happened? Your mom,
that time?"

Eyes glassy, you tucked your chin into your chest. "The

doctors said she was paranoid. Extremely paranoid. She thought... she was sure..." I could barely hear your voice. "I was already dead."

"You? You were with me."

"I know." You explained, keeping your eyes down. The doctors weren't sure what had set your mother off. Maybe it was something she'd read in the paper. Or heard on the radio. Not that it mattered. The point was she got this thing in her head. She was sure she'd discovered a secret way vision could correct itself. The voices began, just a little at first, then every day. All that time you'd thought your mother was okay, a little spacey maybe, she had these voices inside her. The voices told her people were after her, after you. The Mafia or somebody. She was trying to steal their profits. She mustn't leave the house. Not let anyone know where you and your father were. The men with the voices said they'd kill you if she didn't do away with herself first. She did what she did to protect you.

"Me," you said in an angry voice.

You took the stone in your hand and flung it hard. It hung in the air before hitting down. I realized I hadn't seen the brown radio next to your TV for a while.

I wanted to ask, What's it like to have a mother so strange and devoted? A mother whose mind goes away and doesn't always come back? Who you worry about? "Really?" was what fell out of my dry mouth.

"Yeah, she was terrified. About me and my father." You stood up, brushed off your pants. "She's fine now, though."

Early summer, we were at someone else's house, moths buzzing at the window screen. Boys I didn't know were tethered to the stereo with headphones the size of cabbages, two girls sat on the couch watching you. You were sketching whatever appeared in front of you, the orange cat, a black boot flopped over, your own hand holding the charcoal. The girls didn't talk to me. I was there because of you.

"Clear light, Anney," you said, holding out your hand. "Pure acid." The two nearly invisible panes were so small they nearly got lost in your palm.

The acid hit my mind like a hurricane, beating words against the walls of my brain it splintered. Voices began to pull at me like nervous dogs. *Open the door. Here, no here. Hurry why can't you?* I went from room to room, searching for you. I ended up alone in a pink bathtub, sobbing. Everything about me was grotesque, even the fingers growing out of my hands. My mother's voice surfaced. *Why don't you dry up and blow away?* She hated how I wouldn't stop asking her for things, things I knew she wouldn't give. Money, a car, a party after graduation. I began to howl, my voice stretching beyond the bathroom walls.

You came in, made me drink grapefruit juice. "Anne, vitamin C. *Ronnie.* It'll bring you down." The ice seared from throat to breastbone.

Around dawn, green light flowed calmly through the window. My body moved, found you at the bottom of the stairs, staring at the cat, your hand in midair. "She wants to bite me. Sometimes I let her." Scratches ran up your arm like bloody exclamation points. I started to cry again.

"Don't," you said. "Let's talk."

I looked down at you, light pooling around your round face.

"Why can't we feel it when someone dies?" I said. "In Vietnam? Next door? Anywhere on earth?" People were dying. People we knew. Bill Maslow had been blown up by a land mine in May. Terrance Smith hanged himself the night before graduation.

"Wow, Anne. Keep going."

"Why doesn't one less person on the earth matter?" I wasn't sure where other people stopped and I began. I felt my bones pushing against my skin. I hated it. Not just the feeling. Acid.

You tilted your head, smiled.

That summer, you were tripping most weekends. I worked, camp counseling days, waitressing at night. I decided money, not drugs, would set me free. I was headed for college in California that fall. You, New York City, art school. Or maybe Boulder. You weren't sure yet. You painted seriously now, alone in your room, canvases stretched as big as doors. Lengths of silk. Gray circles, purple lines running off the edges. Paintings stacked up behind your door. Paintings you didn't show me.

In August, you called. "Come. You've got to. Everyone will be there."

"Who?"

"Jimi Hendrix, The Dead, Canned Heat. Bob is driving his van up. Tons of room."

"I can't get off. A big wedding party is coming in Saturday."

"Drive up after your shift. We can pick out a spot to meet."

"Okay. I'll ask."

"Anne, it'll be so far out. Three days of peace and music."

After I heard the news, I didn't even get in the car. "Thousands, hundreds of thousands, of young people are descending on the Yasgur's farm in upstate New York. The roads are so jammed, most have abandoned their cars and started walking."

After serving chignon-heavy bridesmaids and men in three-piece suits who kept asking for more champagne, I went home and listened to records alone in my room. The Who, Janis Joplin, Ten Years After. I told myself it was better this way. I could hear everything.

Besides, I'd never find you.

When you got back, your mother called. "It's Catherine," she said, her voice concerned. "Would you talk to her? She's not herself." There wasn't a flicker of doubt in my mind about what your mother said. She'd been out of the hospital for nearly two years.

When I walked into your room, you looked like you were floating, breathing in huge breaths of easy air. You were wearing clothes I'd never seen before, an oddly formal man's black vest and ripped cut-offs, your hair was dark with grease. Your eyes looked out at me and the room as if we were shapes that could at any moment get washed away.

"I must have blacked out," you said. "I'm not sure. There are whole parts of days and nights I can't remember. The music was just out there. I couldn't get anywhere near the stage. Too many people. Too much mud. I climbed up on the roof of Bob's van. That's when I saw it."

"What?"

"At the top of stars. How it fits together. Everything."

"Bob told me nobody knew where you'd gone. They spent hours looking. Everyone was scared." Half of me was jealous. You'd left so easily. Nothing, nobody holding you back. The other half, annoyed that you couldn't bother yourself with what other people thought or felt. *Other people* now included me. Your eyes took this in.

"It all worked out, didn't it, Anney? Here I am. Talking to you."

Instead of art school, you left for places I'd never heard of with people I'd never met. I saw you two, maybe three more times, when you were back from Esalen or Banff or Baja or wherever it was you'd been. Your mother padded around the kitchen. I remember staring at the back of her head, the fuzzy line of gray-black hair against pale skin. She brought us tea in china cups and disappeared into the dining room where the three of us had once sat. This time I kept quiet. I knew by then words could slice open the ugly under-belly of things, raise a stink in the room. You and I talked about how humid it was, Dylan's new album. At some point you told me your father hadn't lived there for a while.

Your mother was relieved, you said. *Really.* Your grand-father had money enough for the both of you. I told you I was a hostess at Denny's. When you looked confused, I said, "It's a restaurant. After classes, I don an orange uniform and cite four kinds of coupon specials." We laughed, and for a moment, time stepped back. Then our conversation spun, never quite took hold.

My husband calls you my old hippie friend.

"What do you mean her name is Catherine?" he says, stretching his big arm up. "Didn't she come back from Woodstock as Rainbow or Forest or something?"

I've never mentioned I called you Mike, and Cath. Never told him what happened to your mother that afternoon. What he likes to remember is how you spent hours lying on top of a VW camper staring at the stars, letting Shankar and the Who soak in. He even bought the album. My husband didn't go to Woodstock either. He was working in Salinas that summer, loading lettuce on trucks.

Do you remember the last time we talked it was on the phone? A couple years later, maybe. I was home visiting my family that summer, my first vacation after landing the big consulting job in San Francisco. You were back in Chappaqua from Spain where you'd been studying with your guru. I'd heard you and your mother were living in an apartment near town. It was strange to think that our house was now bigger than yours. I stood in my parents' living room, watching light catch in the maple leaves.

"You don't know?" you said, your voice low. "Nobody told you?"

"No."

"My mother died January twentieth, the day after her birthday. The car skidded off the road. An icy patch."

I listened to the sound of running water, plates clinking. My mother was washing dishes in the kitchen next door.

"Nobody's sure exactly what happened," you went on. "Maybe she drove off on purpose."

In the silence that swelled between us, this information worked its way through my body. This time, I thought, no one found her. Alone in the car. Was it over in a flash? I hoped so. Or did a stranger come upon her overturned car, call for an ambulance, the lights spinning, the siren going full blast. Did you hold a service? Or was it a quick burial, just family, snow dusting the ground, ice coating the branches? Did you follow it with a few lines in *The Patent Trader*? So brief my mother missed it. Or else forgot. On the twentieth of January, I was working, surrounded by people I haven't seen now in years. When your mother died, I didn't feel a thing. She was just one less person in the world.

"I'm sorry I wasn't there," I said. I wondered when you got the news. Were you standing in that very room or some foreign phone booth? Did the voice say *Mom* or *mother*, the word *dead*? All these things I wanted to know, questions in my head that I didn't ask.

"It's all right, Anne. No one was." Your voice was calm.

"No, that wasn't—I mean—" Every word that came into my head seemed to be cruel or pointless. Finally I managed, "You. I mean, with you."

I don't remember what else we talked about, who said good-bye first. I had no idea this would be the last time I'd hear your voice outside my head. All I remember is how heavy the phone felt as I laid it down, how the greasy spots from my fingers smeared.

Then you were gone. Completely. For years, I swear. I remember barely remembering you, Ronnie and Mike, the black booth, people's outstretched palms. Mostly girls were interested, ones who truly believed we could tell the future, and who we couldn't help later imitating: "Him? I will? Four kids? You're sure?" We laughed, it felt good. A few boys came forward with questions, too. Not about that. Not about who would live, die, make it home from the war, though that question was there, too, waiting for us. The unknowing us. The night we sat in that booth was just a scratch in time compared to finding your mother the afternoon we'd built it.

When the dreams wouldn't stop coming, I began to write to you. Two or three cheerful, vapid letters in the space of ten months. Letters I carefully sealed and sent to the last of many addresses I'd collected for you, an apartment in Calgary. The letters left my hand, left the house, never came back, but never got answered either. I began to worry there was no one to open them.

Finally, I write you this. This letter. No, not a letter. The truth—everything I never told you—hoping that will bring you back. For you have to come back. I have to know the voices that finally claimed your mother haven't also claimed you.

It's late now. Everyone's in bed, and I should go up, too. Still, I want to imagine you sitting on the sofa downstairs, your fingers grazing its flowery arm. Maybe your hair's a yellow-white now, but still as thick as summer leaves. When we meet, will we speak only of the easy memories, bring out photos of smiling children, of husbands as fine as spring? Or will something else press through the fog of years? Your mother's eyes spinning with smoke, the comfort of her chained glasses, the upside-down station wagon? Our faces pointed at the moon? Maybe you'll say she wasn't crazy. Just sad. I feel sad, too. It was your palm we practiced on, remember? I propped your mother's big book in front of us, showed you the fleshy line that gave you years. Many more than forty-nine.

Maybe you'll call me Ronnie. Maybe you'll say it all worked out, didn't it? She's okay now, my mother. Can't you feel it? She's where she needs to be. Not here, her eclipsing eyes, streaming flesh, her mouth moving, no words. She's not between us. There's only you and me here in my living room. Those voices, that's the two of us talking.

ACKNOWLEDGEMENTS

My deep gratitude to Jaynie Royal, Editor of Regal House Publishing, who plucked this manuscript out of her immense slush pile and enthusiastically wanted to publish it. Jaynie—and the entire Regal House team—have been meticulous editors.

Heartfelt thanks to the Leporines writing group—especially Alia Volz and Jackie Doyle—who read draft after draft of this work, simultaneously encouraging and challenging me as the bunnies played around our feet. Many thanks to friends and fellow writers who read early incarnations of these stories: Dan Coshnear, Andy Couturier, Dorothy Hale, Linda Lancione, Lily Iona MacKenzie, Barbara Roether, Mike Shaler, Elizabeth Stark, Susan St. Aubin, and the two Tims: Crandle and Rien.

Immense appreciation to my professors at the University of San Francisco, in particular Aaron Shurin who so impressed me at a Saturday morning information session that I threw caution to the wind, left corporate life, and followed my dreams of becoming a writer; and to Deborah Lichtman whose generosity of spirit and administrative acumen helped me every step along the way.

Catherine Brady's masterful stories and gifted teaching have endlessly inspired me. Thank you.

My wholehearted appreciation to Joshua Mohr—the amazing writer that he is—for saying, "Don't just write a story, Laurie. Write a book!"

Nina Schuyler has been an invaluable reader and mentor. Her careful attention to everything from small details to big questions of meaning has meant the world to me.

Special thanks to Liz McDonough who hired me a decade ago to teach at the UC Berkeley Extension Writing Programs. The dedication and insight of my students over the years have not only made me a stronger teacher, but a better writer, too.

I owe a debt of gratitude to the Community of Writers at Squaw Valley, Tin House, and Lit Camp for support, fellowship, and parties that went way too late.

The San Francisco Writers Grotto offered encouragement, community, and wisdom when I needed them most. Thanks especially to Vanessa Hua, Lee Kravetz, Julie Lythcott-Haims, Ethel Rohan, and Louise Nayer for your expert advice and unfailing support.

I feel profoundly grateful to the following literary journals who published earlier versions of these stories: "Ask for Hateman" in *The Los Angeles Review*, "Bigger Than Life" in *Jabberwock Review* (Nancy D. Hargrove Fiction Prize finalist), "Breathe" in *Timber Magazine*, "Or Best Offer" in *Arroyo Literary Review*, "Restraint" in *Midway Journal*, and "Voices" in *Dogwood: A Journal of Poetry and Prose* (Fiction Prize finalist). KY Story Press anthologized "Or Best Offer," and Stories on Stage Sacramento honored this piece with a delightful dramatic reading.

To my family and friends: your pride and faith have sustained me. I'm especially grateful to my father for teaching me honesty and perseverance, two qualities at the heart of my writing.

A huge hug to my son Marco, *mijo, mi cielo,* who in more ways than he knows gave me the courage to write these stories. Thank you, Marquito, for being just who you are.

No one deserves more thanks than my husband Sam. He selflessly supported every word I wrote in this book.

My deepest appreciation to him for proofing drafts, shopping and doing the laundry when I was too exhausted, and driving Marco back and forth so I could finish just one more sentence, try out one more ending. Thank you one million times over.